P. M. Hubbard and Th ⌐. ꓵoom

》》 This title is part of The Murder Room, our series dedicated to making available out-of-print or hard-to-find titles by classic crime writers.

Crime fiction has always held up a mirror to society. The Victorians were fascinated by sensational murder and the emerging science of detection; now we are obsessed with the forensic detail of violent death. And no other genre has so captivated and enthralled readers.

Vast troves of classic crime writing have for a long time been unavailable to all but the most dedicated frequenters of second-hand bookshops. The advent of digital publishing means that we are now able to bring you the backlists of a huge range of titles by classic and contemporary crime writers, some of which have been out of print for decades.

From the genteel amateur private eyes of the Golden Age and the femmes fatales of pulp fiction, to the morally ambiguous hard-boiled detectives of mid twentieth-century America and their descendants who walk our twenty-first century streets, The Murder Room has it all. 》》

The Murder Room
Where Criminal Minds Meet

themurderroom.com

P. M. Hubbard (1910–1980)

Praised by critics for his clean prose style, characterization, and the strong sense of place in his novels, Philip Maitland Hubbard was born in Reading, in Berkshire and brought up in Guernsey, in the Channel Islands. He was educated at Oxford, where he won the Newdigate Prize for English verse in 1933. From 1934 until its disbandment in 1947 he served with the Indian Civil service. On his return to England he worked for the British Council, eventually retiring to work as a freelance writer. He contributed to a number of publications, including *Punch*, and wrote 16 novels for adults as well as two children's books. He lived in Dorset and Scotland, and many of his novels draw on his interest in and knowledge of rural pursuits and folk religion.

Flush as May
Picture of Millie
A Hive of Glass
The Holm Oaks
The Tower
The Custom of the Country
Cold Waters
High Tide
The Dancing Man
A Whisper in the Glen
A Rooted Sorrow
A Thirsty Evil
The Graveyard
The Causeway
The Quiet River
Kill Claudio

The Tower

P. M. Hubbard

An Orion book

Copyright © Caroline Dumonteil, Owain Rhys Phillips and Maria
Marcela Appleby Gomez 1967, 2012

The right of P. M. Hubbard to be identified as the author of this work
has been asserted in accordance with the Copyright, Designs and
Patents Act 1988.

This edition published by
The Orion Publishing Group Ltd
Orion House
5 Upper St Martin's Lane
London WC2H 9EA

An Hachette UK company
A CIP catalogue record for this book is available from the British Library

ISBN 978 1 4719 0085 3

www.orionbooks.co.uk

CHAPTER 1

THE CAR was running easily downhill, and the engine stopped working so quietly and suddenly that at first he did not notice it had happened. Then as the slope eased for a moment he felt the car check, and saw the red light shining wickedly at him from the dial of the speedometer. He said, "Oh damn," put his foot on the brake, thought better of it and let the car run on in neutral.

It was dusk even on the tops of the hills and down in the trees below him quite dark. There were lights among the trees. It looked like a village, but he did not know what its name was. All he knew was that ahead of him, another twenty miles along the road, there was a town called Frantham with a two-star pub called the Antelope. Two stars was about his mark on this trip.

A gaggle of signs came up suddenly in his not over-bright headlights. They said first COYLE and then BEND and NARROW BRIDGE. He noted, but did not like, the name, negotiated the bend without having to use his brakes and saw the hump of the bridge ahead. The car checked at the slope, and he found himself sitting forward, like a horseman at a jump, trying to ease her over the obstacle. She got her nose between the parapet walls, crawled up the slope with unexpected momentum, paused, dipped and began to gather speed on the far side.

The hood was down, and he heard, in the suddenly almost motionless air about his head, the rush of a considerable stream below the bridge. Then the road leveled out and the car came

1

gradually but inexorably to a halt. He turned off the headlights and sat there. His mind, as always after a long drive, was numb and unresponsive. The emergencies of movement it could cope with, but not the emergency of sudden stoppage. He said, "Damn" again, and shivered slightly.

Ahead, beyond the faint yellowish glow of the sidelights, he could just see the tarmac picking up the last of the light in the sky. It was dark on both sides with what looked like trees. He sat there wrapped in the inertia of mild despair. The stream was some way behind him now, and the silence was absolute. He shivered again, and suddenly found himself cold and stiff.

Then, not ten yards ahead of him, a voice said, "Oh God, oh God," and started to weep. He considered for a moment joining in the general lamentation, but came to the conclusion that the situation did not warrant it. It did not, to be honest, matter whether he reached Frantham tonight. Or even, he thought, to-morrow night or the night after. There might even be a pub in Coyle with attractions rivaling those of the Antelope. And some-one else, at least, was unhappier than he was. He opened the door quietly and got out.

He reached into the chaos behind the driving seat, found his duffel coat and put it on. Thus wrapped, he felt better equipped to deal with what appeared, at the moment, to be a purely social problem. He wanted to ask for help. But could he decently ask help of someone who seemed, at least in his own judgment, to be more in need of help himself? If the weeper had been a woman, a sense of gallantry, or at worse a sense of opportunist adventure, might have driven him to offer help, even from his own position of relative helplessness. But he did not think it was. Admittedly, men, when they cried, cried higher than they talked. A childish response seemed to activate naturally a forgot-ten childishness in the vocal chords. Admittedly, too, a man did not often weep audibly on a dark country roadside, even in a

2

village with a name like Coyle. He still thought, on balance, that it was a man weeping.

He began to walk slowly forward, and was at once aware that it would be impossible, in this dark desolation, to tiptoe tactfully past a fellow creature in distress and seek help elsewhere. The words "Can I help?" formed themselves in his mind. It was what, a minute or so ago, he would have liked some solid and mechanically minded passer-by to say to him. He walked on cautiously and, now that he came to think of it, quietly, as quietly as he could go. Then he found that the weeping had stopped.

He stopped himself and listened. Now that his ears were attuned to the silence, he could hear, very faint behind him, the murmur of the stream. Some way ahead, where the lights would have been, a voice called "Good night" cheerfully, and a door slammed. Coyle was not, as he had somehow felt it might be, steeped in universal distress. But at hand there was nothing. No voice, no breath, no movement. This at least made his decision easier. Indeed, it left no problem for a decision. You cannot offer to help, nor need you tactfully avoid, a person who on the evidence is no longer there. He gathered his coat around him and stepped out for the village.

He had not gone twenty yards before he found that he was walking slightly but definitely downhill. Twenty yards pushing on the level, and the car would be moving again. It was a heavy car for its size by modern standards, but well within his capacity on anything but a pronounced upgrade. He hesitated and then walked on. Better see, first, what the village consisted of and where he should head for. The main thing was to get the car off the road, where he could turn the lights off. He did not trust his battery an inch. If he was going to slide silently into Coyle, pulled on by gravity but pushed by himself or nothing, he must have an exact destination.

The houses came up very suddenly, first on one side of the

3

road and then on the other. There were lights in some of them, but very faint and far back, as if the occupants were all in their back kitchens or, in the front, crouched over their television screens. Then the road turned and he saw, high up on his right, a sign which said THE BELL. It was dimly lit, and the gold paint on the picture looked cracked and tarnished. His heart sank, but at the same moment he saw, at the side of the house, a tall stone arch with the darkness of what looked like a yard behind it. Even here there were next to no lights. He thought he could hear, not far off, the intermittent murmur of voices, but he could not tell where they came from.

He stopped at the archway and peered in. There was indeed a yard at the side of the house. There were dustbins on one side, along the end wall of the house, and what looked like garages on the other. This would do for a start. He turned and began walking back to the car. He padded quietly along in his soft shoes, and heard, hard and clear on the tarmac, other feet, more substantially shot, coming to meet him. They walked slowly but not, he thought, hesitantly. If this was the weeper, the man had wept it out of himself, and was coming back with reasonable resolution to face whatever it was in Coyle that had set him weeping. From the security of his comparative silence, he got ready for the encounter.

Silence or no silence, the other man saw him first. A voice said, "Ah—? Ah, good evening." It was a warm voice, but light and medium-pitched. He tried to connect it with the desolation of "Oh God, oh God" by the dark roadside, but could not be sure either way. He said, "Good evening," and only then his motorist's eyes picked out the broad shape coming up to him out of the darkness. He shortened stride, expecting further speech and ready with his hard-luck story about the car, but the other man did not stop. Still slowly, but unremittingly, the metaled heels came down on the tarmac, and the man was past him and

4

off toward the village.

The lights of the car looked orange-yellow and secretive. He leaned in and switched them off, conscious even in the enveloping darkness that there was a law in Coyle and that he was defying it. He took off his coat and threw it on to the driving seat. Then he put one hand on the wheel, leaned his shoulder against the side of the windscreen and started to push. With the car aggressively immobile, he had not bothered to put on the hand brake.

Another voice, this time distinctly feminine, said, "She'll go, you know, if you'd rather."

He said, "Good lord. Will she? Why?"

"It was a distributor lead. They jump off."

He said again, "Good lord. Is that what they do?"

"Well anyway, this one did."

"And you put it back on?"

"Uh-huh." There was a figure now, pale and somehow suspended a foot or two off the ground. A spirit, he decided, but a benign one.

He said, "That's very nice of you."

"Think nothing of it. Good night."

He hesitated, and then, finding nothing else to say, said "Good night" and got into the car. The engine started at a touch. He switched on the lights and saw, lit faintly in their reflected glow, a girl watching him. She was perched owl-like on the top of what looked like a milestone, her knees drawn up almost under her chin. She looked as if she had been there for hours and was still perfectly comfortable. There was no detail in the picture.

He put the car in gear and started off for Frantham. But when he came to the Bell, he braked and swung the car through the archway into the yard. He switched off the engine, turned the lights off and went around to the front door of the pub. Even inside the light was no more than yellow. There were three doors, one ahead, unmarked, one on the left marked SALOON and one on the right marked PUBLIC. He put his hand to the PUBLIC door and, as it started to open, heard a voice inside say, "He says, bugger you, he says, I'll bloody well do what I please, and you can fucking well do the same, that's what he says."

The voice was low and distinct against a background of dead silence. He pictured two men talking, one behind the bar and one in front of it. He opened the door wide on a room full of smoke and beer fumes, and then saw in the faint light that it was also full of bodies. They sat everywhere, on benches, on settles, on chairs drawn up at tables. None of them moved. Only the landlord was on his feet, leaning motionless on the bar with his shirt sleeves rolled up to the elbows, impassively presiding. He turned his eyes as the door opened, but answered the man who had spoken. He said, "It's nasty, that, having a chap talk like that." He turned his head to follow his eyes and said, "Good evening." No one else, apparently, moved at all, except for the eyes. He felt himself suddenly caught and held in a blank concentration of eyes.

He said, "Good evening. I suppose—can you by any chance let me have a room for the night?"

The landlord looked at him speculatively. "We've got a room," he said. "You got a car?" He said it almost as if he was about to suggest an exchange of amenities.

"I put it in the yard."

The landlord nodded. "I'll tell my wife," he said. "If you'll go in the saloon?" He made it sound like a courtesy.

"Right." He nodded, backed out and shut the door of the public bar behind him. No one else had moved or spoken. The saloon smelled of polished linoleum. It was dim, spotless and quite empty. A small red-faced woman appeared suddenly behind the varnished bar in the right-hand corner. "Good evening," she said. "You'll be staying over?"

6

"If I may. I was going on to Frantham, but I think I've come far enough for the night." He did not say, even to himself, that he wanted to know what made men weep in the roadside trees and girls who could mend cars sit like owls on the top of milestones. The woman produced a book and opened it on the bar. "If you'll just register," she said.

He produced a ball-point from his jacket pocket and wrote, "John Smith, Ashby-de-la-Zouche, British." She watched him as he wrote, and he felt an overpowering urge to tell her that he really was John Smith. Someone had to be. She nodded. "Single?" she said.

"Oh yes, quite single." That was the trouble with John Smith. They always expected you to bring in a giggling blonde with the wrong initials on her suitcase.

"I'll see to the room," she said. She turned to go and then stopped. "Have you had your supper?" she said.

"Well, no. I—"

She nodded. "Bacon and eggs do?"

"Oh yes, fine. And could I have a pint of bitter?"

He sat back on the polished settle, pulling slowly at his tankard and letting his mind clear. He could not make out whether the dreamlike quality of his recent experience lay in the experience itself or in the daze of the recording consciousness. In any case, why worry? It was on the whole pleasant, after a long drive, to let the unreasonableness of facts take care of itself, and simply to contemplate it, placidly and impassively, while the alcohol laid healing hands on his raw nerves. It was, he decided, very strong beer, and no harm in that. As a further sign of emancipation, he yawned suddenly and deeply. Given the promised eggs and bacon, he could safely let go. With the morning light he would reconsider the evidence. The part of his mind that refused to be comforted asked whether the sun ever really rose over Coyle, or whether the village lived permanently in a soft and dimly lit darkness, through which people moved oddly without explanation. But the question remained unanswered.

The eggs and bacon, when they arrived, assumed the proportions less of a soporific than of a general anesthetic. He pushed the last pale slice of bread and butter around his plate, mopping up the rich brown grease, and wondered whether he could ever rouse himself to get his things out of the car. The voices in the public bar, which he had been dimly aware of as he ate, swelled suddenly into argument. There was some shouting and intermittent swearing against a background of rolling waves of laughter. He could not tell at all what it was all about, but nothing in any case could have prepared him for the way it ended.

A man started to sing, casually, as if he was singing to himself, but loud enough to be heard above the general uproar. "*Gloria Deo—*" he sang, with a long twisting run of notes on the rounded *o* of the first syllable. Two more voices took it up in different parts, a very sweet clear tenor led the way into *Et Filio*, and by the time *Sancto* was reached he counted four parts going great guns with several voices to each. There was a second's silence and then the whole lot came in together with *Sicut in principio*, and suddenly, unbelievably, a piercing falsetto, harshly vibrant but bang on the note, soared up in a tremendous counter-tenor descant, that hung about under the smoke-laden ceiling joists until it came toppling down to join the consort in a long-drawn unison *Amen*.

There was a second's breathless silence, and then a roar of cheers and laughter. Benches were pushed back, drained tankards came down with bangs on the bare tabletops, and the company began to bid each other good night. The landlord came through behind the bar, his hands full of empties, and apologized for the noise. John Smith shook his head at him and got slowly to his feet.

"Ready for bed?" the landlord said. "I'll get my wife to show you the room."

8

John nodded and went out to the car. He pulled the hood over but did not screw down the clamps. His suitcase seemed unreasonably heavy as he lifted it out. The night was full of boots on tarmac, and someone started up a car farther down the road. A man went past the archway, telling his companion that he'd be buggered if he did something that John could not catch. It was all idiotically familiar and breathlessly unreal. He went back into the yellow light of the doorway, lugging his heavy suitcase.

The room was papered with rustic trellises, in which colored birds perched at predictable intervals among a repetitive profusion of seed-catalogue blossom. The window was curtained and he did not look out.

It was the bells, ultimately, that woke him, a cascade of regimented sound that got in everywhere and would not let him sleep. He groaned, turned over and looked at his watch. It was half past seven and, as he now remembered, Sunday. The bells went on remorselessly, slipping through their changes with unhesitant precision at what seemed breakneck speed. He got out of bed, yanked aside the heavy curtains and blinked at the somehow unexpected daylight. Right opposite him, buttressed, crenelated and pinnacled, the church tower filled the foreground against a backcloth of banked trees. Motionless and unrevealing, it looked at him from behind the drooped eyelids of its elaborate louvers and poured out its staggering profusion of sound.

John Smith shook his head at it and reached for his dressing gown. He wondered if there was any chance, anywhere, of a cup of tea.

CHAPTER 2

"I'VE MADE A pot of tea for myself," the landlord said. "If you'd like a cup—" He looked at it doubtfully, as though it was in some way unfit for general consumption. "My wife will be back directly. If you'd like to wait—"

John said, "I'd like one very much," and the landlord shrugged. "Help yourself," he said. He pushed over the teapot and a cup and saucer. The dark brew had oily streaks in it which the thick yellow milk only threw up in a livelier iris. There was a grievance here somewhere, John thought. He wondered whether to fish for it or pretend not to notice it. A publican's wife who went to church at eight on a Sunday morning might well, he could see, be a professional liability as well as something of a social curiosity. He made a very delicate cast over where he judged the grievance lay. "You've got wonderful bell-ringers here," he said.

The landlord raised his eyebrows but kept his eyes in his cup. "Oh yes," he said. "Won a prize of some sort, they did, last year. There was that festival they went over for." He spoke with elaborate detachment, like an orthodox Levite discussing the goings-on at High Places with a stranger who might turn out to be a Babylonian. John dropped his fly somewhat more heavily on the same spot. "Do they ring again for eleven o'clock?" he said.

The lurking grievance made a tentative snap at it. "They do," the landlord said. "And again for six." He raised his eyes and gave John a quick appraising glance. "Can't hear yourself think on a Sunday," he said, "not in Coyle."

John nodded and sipped his tea. He doubted whether his hostess's tea, when she returned, would in any case be any great improvement. Whatever you did, the mischief was in the tea tin.

The landlord looked at him more thoroughly. "You'll be wanting your breakfast," he said. There was no question in it. It was an assertion which he dared John to deny. He went on quickly, leaving no room for denial, even if one was contemplated. "You'll get it when my wife gets back," he said. He put his cup in the sink and looked gloomily through the doorway into the stale chaos of the Public Bar. He sighed. "When she's got her hat off," he said. He went through into the bar and set about it. John got up from the edge of the kitchen table, looked apprehensively through the door of the bar and tiptoed to the sink. The window over the sink looked out on to a rather dingy back yard with something like a wash house on the far side. It was quite impossible to pretend that there was anything to keep him there. With a quick guilty gesture he swilled his tea into the sink and put his cup down quietly beside his host's. Then he went upstairs to dress.

The landlord's name, he saw, was George Curtis. He had a full license, but from what John had seen, most of his trade was in the beer. He wandered out into the road and looked about him. There was nothing wrong with Coyle to look at. The houses were stone and slate and set well back. The woodwork was mostly freshly painted. The side lanes, one in front of him and one farther to his right, made neat right angles with the central street. He noticed, as a sign of grace, that there was no street lighting. The morning was cloudy but bright. There was not a soul about.

He pottered across the road and into the lane opposite. It would be called Church Lane but, as a further sign of grace, did not say so. He saw simultaneously, at the end of the lane ahead of him, the south side of the church tower and, dwarfed by it but still very prominent, an elaborately painted notice board headed *Appeal*.

Money, he thought, the usual thing. The vast, nagging up-keep of an ancient building in traditional materials which only the experts could handle nowadays. And the dwindling company of the faithful. Or in most places, anyhow. Here he wondered. It was the tower they wanted money for. He read on and whistled. Twenty thousand pounds. Twenty thousand pounds, by the Lord Harry. He looked at the tower with fresh interest. Something was wrong with it. Not structurally, from what he could see from here, though that too, presumably. But something in its looks. The proportions were wrong, and the detail at the top was too much for the noble simplicity of the foot. Bad restoration probably. But all some way back.

"Eighteen-eighty," the man said. He was a short, broad, powerful man, with a bare head of self-consciously snowy hair. He seemed to have appeared from a path leading left-handed around the west side of the churchyard, but John, intent on the tower, had not seen or heard him come.

John nodded gloomily. "Worst time," he said. "Do you know everything about me, or only what I'm thinking?"

The broad man smiled. He was immensely friendly and almost embarrassingly conscious of his staggering charm. "Not your name," he said. "I know you're staying at the Bell. Oh— and the number and make of your car."

John nodded. "John Smith," he said. "Really," he added.

"Yes?" the man said. "Yes, well I don't see why not. The combination must occur."

"It does. Try the London telephone directory. Or any telephone directory, for that matter. It doesn't really simplify things as it should."

"No. No, I can see that. One knows, of course, that children called Gavin Dalrymple grow up into Gavin Dalrymples and behave accordingly. But I suppose it works the other way too. Do you suffer from a sort of claustrophobic aggressiveness?" He looked at John with friendly interest. "You don't look aggressive," he said. "My name," he added, "is Charles Hardcastle. A fair *via media*, don't you think?"

John, conscious of no small charm of his own, smiled back at him. "You don't look median to me," he said. "Compensation, perhaps? Overcompensation for Charles?"

"You don't bandy cheap psychology for a living, do you?"

"Good God, no. I am supposed to apply it, but that's all my eye. I explain things for a living. We had all the jargon thrown at us during an unusually laborious and useless training course. But in fact all one needs is the gift of the gab and a lot of elaborately concealed patience."

"What do you explain, then?"

"Systems. Efficiency without tears. Organization and method stuff. My firm sells it and I go and show the customers how it works."

"And they pay you for this?"

"Oh yes. They pay me quite well, I think."

Mr. Hardcastle shook his head. "Admirable," he said. "But not in Coyle, surely?"

"No, no. I'm just passing through. I've been on holiday, in fact, but the money ran out a bit sooner than I expected, and I'm rather limping home."

"I tell you what," said Mr. Hardcastle, "come to breakfast. You won't get it at the Bell yet."

"I know. Not until Mrs. Curtis has got her hat off."

"No, that's it, do you see. So come and have it with me, why not? Up there." He nodded toward the church tower, and John had a momentary vision of coffee and toast between the crenela-

13

tions. Then he saw what it was. Among the trees that swept up behind the church there was the intermittent outline of a house. It was built of pale brick and looked long and low. "Thank you very much," he said. "I'd better tell Mr. Curtis."

"Don't worry. I'll ring him." Mr. Hardcastle turned and walked off along the flagged path, and John followed. "What did they do?" he said. "Diddle it up with all that fancy work? It doesn't look— I couldn't quite make it out."

"No. They built it up, don't you see? A whole new stage. They used to ring from the floor of the church like Christians, with a nice straightforward bell-chamber on top. I've got a picture somewhere. I'll show you. But that wasn't good enough for the eighties. They put the ringers in the bell-chamber and stuck a new bell-chamber on top of that. The detail, of course, followed. Even the stone's different, do you see? Hence the appeal."

The path began to climb on broad shallow steps of stone. They were already nearly level with the nave roof. Shrubbery closed in on both sides between the treetrunks, and they came to a white-painted gate. It had the name GALEHANGER on it. Mr. Hardcastle nodded at it apologetically. "The twenties, I'm afraid. The beginning of the local place-name cult. Before your time, of course. They stopped calling new roads after local councillors and called them by the old field names. They're still at it— especially the new towns. It's the wood, of course. It's the Gale hanger. If a Coyle boy says to a Coyle girl, 'I'll meet you in the Gale,' he doesn't mean *High Wind in Jamaica* stuff. He means up in the woods. Where they always have. Half the people in Coyle must have been got in the Gale. Well—not half, perhaps. Nearly all the first-born. You know what it is."

John said, "Milk Wood?"

"That's right. Then just before the planners got a grip, a chap came along and got the owner to carve him out a slice of wood

14

to build a house in. Wouldn't be allowed now, of course. Quite right, too. But it's a lovely position. Look."

They had come out on to a flagged terrace with a low stone wall all along the southern side. Straight across from them, the bedeviled tower stood up unapologetically above the long blue spine of the church roof and the mottled angles of the roofs of Coyle. Its pinnacles and crenelations were still clear above them, and John, taking in the picture with an idle, early-morning appreciation, saw a wisp of movement between them. "There's someone up there," he said.

"Already?" Mr. Hardcastle looked at his watch. "Could be, if the congregation wasn't too large. He goes up there after the service."

"Who?"

"Oh—the vicar, of course. Old Liberty. Freeman, his name is. Father Freeman, he calls himself. He is, too. Got a son married over in Carshot. Nice chap. The son, I mean. That was before he had the call, of course."

John turned back from his contemplation of the tower. "I'm sorry," he said. "I wasn't concentrating. What was?"

"Oh—the son, I mean. He wouldn't do it now, not Father Freeman. He's all for the celibacy of the clergy. I try to resist the temptation to tell him he's had the best of both worlds. That's too easy. He's perfectly honest. According to his lights. That's why it all works as it does."

John shook his head. "Sorry, again. What works?"

"Well, the parish. St. Udan's, Coyle."

"I see, yes. The bell-ringers. And the choir, my goodness, of course. And indeed Mrs. Curtis's hat."

"And indeed Mrs. Curtis's hat. As for the bells—well, you can imagine. From here. But it's all high jinks, and they enjoy it no end." He paused. "It's very medieval, really. There's the opposition, of course. Well—you've seen George Curtis, I've no doubt,

15

mopping out his bar single-handed on a Sunday morning. Old Liberty thinks I'm leader of the opposition. Antichrist in person. I'm not, really. I'm a neutral. As a humanist, I like to see the fun. Come and see what there is for breakfast."

John could see at once that the house was going to be an extraordinarily pleasant one. It was in a medium, between-wars tradition of domestic architecture, which had got over both imitation antiques and overstuffedness, but not yet caught the full wind of modernity. It had something of a Georgian, or at least neo-Georgian, simplicity. Mr. Hardcastle led him into a dining room with a breakfast table laid for two. He opened a serving hatch and put his head through. "Mrs. Mallet," he called, "an extra for breakfast. All right? I'll lay for him. Oh—and will you phone Mr. Curtis and tell him his guest is here?"

Somewhere far back a voice said something, and he took his head out of the hatch. He went to the sideboard and took out mats and cutlery. "Sit down," he said. He nodded at the place already laid.

John said, "Won't your wife—?"

"I haven't got a wife. Not now. It's my daughter. But her breakfasts are always a bit unpredictable."

The hatch opened and a third set of crockery appeared, followed by food and coffee. They began to eat, but still no third person joined them.

"About the tower," said John.

"Well, what I said. They clapped this extra bit on top and hung the bells in it. They never apparently gave a thought to the foundations and lower walls. They carried the buttresses up further, but of course that's just eyewash. Well—it might have been all right, I suppose. There might well have been a factor of safety in the original job capable of carrying this extra load. But in point of fact there wasn't. It's been giving way, gradually, for years now. The foundations have sunk and the lower walls

16

are out of winding. They've been patched up, of course. Filling the cracks, that's all. But it can't go on, or they'll have the whole thing down on top of them. Hence, as I say, the appeal."

"Twenty thousand. I saw. They can't get it, can they?"

"Of course they can't get it. And the point is, it's not necessary. The proper job wouldn't cost half that. That's why they can't get help from the central funds."

"The proper job being—"

"Well, obviously—back to 1870. Take the bells out, take off all that damned spiky superstructure, rehang the bells where they belong and Triple Bob's your uncle. That's oversimplifying, of course. There's got to be work done underneath now. But nothing unreasonable. And of course the improvement in appearance would be spectacular. I must show you that picture. It's a good tower, that, as originally built."

"Then what's the twenty thousand for?" John found himself, with the back half of his mind, wondering whether Mr. Hardcastle was the sort of man to have a daughter who perched on milestones. With the front half he listened politely.

"To make it safe as it is. An enormous job, even if they can do it properly, which I doubt. Underpinning the foundations, even jacking them up, for all I know, steel reinforcements, God knows what else. It's lunatic, of course."

John came to the conclusion that Mr. Hardcastle's daughter might be expected, in reason, to do almost anything. He said, "Then why—?"

"Old Liberty. He won't have it. Oh, hullo, Cynthia. This is Mr. John Smith. He really is John Smith. He is full of compensatory aggressions."

John, on his feet with his chair pushing at the back of his knees, could not be certain. There was too little to go on. But if there was another girl who mended cars, Miss Hardcastle would do very well as a bonus issue. She showed no sign of recognition.

17

She flicked a pair of green eyes at him as she made for the food on the sideboard. "How do you do, Mr. Smith?" she said. The voice could be the same. But it was difficult to see this girl roosting. There was, apart from anything else, too much of her. Not too much for other purposes—never that. Only for roosting. But he still did not know. He said, "How do you do, Miss Hardcastle?" and hung, poised, while she poked about among the dishes.

"Sit down," she said, "please. Otherwise I'll go and pick the wrong thing and feel bad about it afterwards. There seems an awful lot left. Has Daddy given you a proper breakfast?"

"I've done excellently."

"Well, come and get some more when you're ready. Have you been having the phallic symbols?"

"I don't think so. Unless you count—I had bacon and sausages."

"No, I mean the tower. That's what you were talking about, weren't you? I wondered if Daddy had been giving you the phallic-symbol treatment."

"No, I—"

"Well, that's a good sign. He only does it to shock. And that always means—"

Mr. Hardcastle said, "Mr. Smith is quite unshockable. So don't you try it either. We were talking sensibly, and you've interrupted us. Why can't you come down at the proper time? You can't have overslept. Not on a Sunday in Coyle. No one could."

Cynthia said, "No, but I was tired. I was out late." She lifted a pale, heart-shaped face and looked at John with a sort of serious candor. She was giving nothing away. He still did not know, but found her extremely disturbing.

John said, "You were saying the vicar wouldn't have it. I mean, wouldn't have the tower cut down to size."

"That's right. Nor he will. He won't see it's all wrong as it is. They've all told him. Including the diocesan architect. But he's

18

got the Church Council in his pocket, and it's for them to decide. All the diocese can do is refuse to help. Which, as I say, they have. So he's out on his own, gunning for his twenty thousand."

"Which he can't get?"

"No. Well—there's one conceivable source. But he hasn't succeeded in tapping it yet. Meanwhile—"

"Meanwhile the tower is on point of collapse?"

"I don't know that, of course. Nobody does. No, I was going to say, meanwhile he's collecting money with astonishing ingenuity and perseverance from wherever he can lay his hands on it. But of course, not fast enough. I mean, apart from the time factor in the tower itself, costs are rising all the time. Unless we get a really solid deflation, it's going to be as much as he can do to keep level, let alone catch up with his receding target. But you wouldn't think so, to hear him talk."

"But why? What's his objection to the proper job? Or is it sheer obstinacy? I haven't met him, of course."

"You will, if you're here much longer. No. Well, yes, all right. Obstinacy, certainly. But I know what I think. Here, come outside a moment and I'll show you."

Cynthia said, "Let Mr. Smith finish his breakfast before you spring Lady Athaliah on him."

"He can finish his breakfast afterwards. It won't take a moment." He was already out of the door. John and Cynthia exchanged a long glance. It was John who weakened first. "Coming," he said.

Mr. Hardcastle was by the terrace wall. "Look," he said. "You can see where the top ought to be. There's a string-course round the tower now. And the stone changes. Now if that was the top—"

"It's below us."

"That's it. That's it, you see. This house was built long after

19

1880. If the tower came down to its original height now, I'd be sitting on top of it."

"And the vicar won't have that?"

"That's what I think. He's an odd fish. Striking his colors to Antichrist—something of that sort. But more than that, don't you see? He'd be overlooked."

CHAPTER 3

GEORGE CURTIS SAID, "Be staying on a day or two, perhaps?"

"Well," said John, "I don't know. I hadn't really thought. There's no reason why I shouldn't."

"Well, I thought—you being a friend of Mr. Hardcastle—"

"I'm not, actually. I mean—I hadn't met him until this morning. But he was certainly very kind."

"Very nice man, Mr. Hardcastle. Clever, too. Professor or something he was, before they came here. Of course, there's some don't get on with him. He talks too straight for some of them. But he talks sense." He gave John one of his sudden, calculating inspections. "At least, to my way of thinking."

Antichrist, thought John. The leader of the opposition. It's a wonder they don't all wear colors. He said, refusing to be drawn, "Always two sides, aren't there? Especially in a village like this. But I liked him, I must say."

George Curtis said, "That's right," and Mrs. Curtis came into the bar. She said, "It's ready to come in," and he nodded and went out. She did things behind the bar while they both mentally traced the landlord's movements through the kitchen and out of the door to the back yard and whatever it was that needed to come in. Then she said, "Will you be wanting your room again tonight, Mr. Smith?"

John went through an elaborate act of unprepared consideration. He was amused, and slightly horrified, to find himself

21

already so deeply committed. He said, "Oh—I don't know. Yes, I think I might as well, if it's not inconvenient to you."

"Oh, it's not inconvenient." Both the Curtises, John noticed, were adept at piling implications into innocent phrases. "I don't know whether you'd want meals?"

"Well—if you can manage breakfast. And then perhaps bacon and eggs in the evening, if you could. Don't worry about anything else."

"You'll be having meals out, I expect."

"Oh? Well, I always can, anyway. So don't you worry."

A voice said suddenly, "Mrs. Curtis? Mrs. Curtis, are you there?" It was a woman's voice. John, with his eyes on the door through into the kitchen, thought it was the most female voice he had ever heard. The woman appeared suddenly behind the bar, smiling, so that he was flooded by the warmth of her smile before she even seemed to have seen him. He had the idea, seeing her like that, that she was the archetypal barmaid, only no barmaid he had ever seen wore those clothes. Or smelled like that, he thought. It must be something unbelievably expensive, but the effect was that of a natural emanation. Mrs. Curtis said, "Oh, my lady—Mrs. Garstin—I didn't hear you come in." They smiled at each other, the small, red-faced serious woman and this piece of personified high summer, so that John, standing alone on the wrong side of the bar, felt suddenly angular and superfluous. They seemed to be talking parish matters but he hardly followed the drift in his concentration on Mrs. Garstin.

She was without compunction or disguise a middle-aged woman. Or rather, he thought, she had triumphantly surpassed her youth. Whatever had contributed to this result, it did not seem to matter how long it had taken. Or how much it had cost. He remembered afterward that the features were aquiline and clear-cut, but the whole face small. He could not swear to her coloring, only the almost visible glow which radiated from her.

She said, "All right, Mrs. Curtis. I just thought I'd look in and make sure." She swung her smile around like a lighthouse beam, very slowly. It caught John and held him for a moment, as it had when she came in; then there was only her back. She said, "Don't bother to come out." She disappeared through the door into the kitchen, and Mrs. Curtis bustled after her. John put down his tankard and moved, without thinking what he was doing, to the window, flattening his nose on the glass to watch her get into the long, dark-blue car. When he turned, he found George Curtis watching him from behind the bar. There was the ghost of a smile on his face, but it was at least half the smile of a fellow conspirator. In their mere masculinity they were in this together.

The landlord said, "That's Mrs. Garstin." The information he conveyed was solely about himself. John nodded but found nothing intelligent to say. "Used to be Lady Potter until she married Mr. Garstin. Out at Upsindon." He jerked his head westward. "Big place. Comes down as far as the river on this side. He was their agent in Sir Gerald's time, Mr. Garstin was." For no very apparent reason he sighed, mopping with his cloth along the spotless top of the bar, his eyes fixed on John's. "But he's a nice man, Mr. Garstin."

That makes two of them, John thought. Two nice men in George Curtis's local world. He wondered what they had in common, Mr. Hardcastle, who had only a daughter, and Mr. Garstin, who was married to this woman you caught your breath at and ran to the window to watch getting into her car. Wherever George Curtis had built his mental fence, they were both on the right side of it. And himself, he hoped. He did not at all know why, but he badly wanted to qualify for niceness. He said, "Have they been here long?"

"Some time now. Some time before Sir Gerald died, even, and that's going on seven years." He looked at John again with that slightly puzzled, lost look, as though he somehow needed reassurance, but did not see much hope of getting it. "And I'd known Mr. Garstin before ever he came here. Almost since he was a boy. I worked for his father over at Ganstock. Before I went into the trade, of course, that was." He smiled at something he did not explain. "You couldn't help liking him," he said. "But that's how it goes, isn't it?"

He went through into the kitchen, trundling a rubber-tired trolley, on which he carried the empty metal drum which he had now, no doubt, replaced with a full one. John, vaguely discomforted, finished his beer and went out into the street. He looked up and down, but saw nothing and nobody likely to answer the questions he had hardly formulated but wanted answered. He crossed the street and went along Church Lane. When he came to the end of it, he looked hopefully along the flagged path leading off to his left. But this time no one had come down to meet him, and the long house, tucked back among the trees of the Gale, looked blindly at him from over the church roof. He sighed and went in through the elaborate lych gate. George Curtis had sighed. Something to do with Mr. Garstin and his marriage. Mr. Garstin had married his boss's widow. But he was a nice man. That was it—the sigh and then the but.

He pushed open the heavy door, noticing vaguely that it was very shiny and well cared for, and went into the church. Only his ineradicable reverence, which he felt to the accumulated holiness of the place rather than an identifiable God, prevented him from whistling. St. Udan's, Coyle, was got up to kill. There was color everywhere, brilliant primary colors picked out with gilding and put on in niggling detail with great care and skill. It reminded him of fairground machinery and showmen's caravans, or the bedizened brilliance of the prenationalization canal boats. He said under his breath, "Folk art, by golly," and tiptoed into the nave.

Most of the windows were white glass and had been left so.

24

The east window of the chancel was a war memorial of the Kaiser's war, done in the tasteful, washed-out colors of the twenties. It looked incredibly out of place. And cheap, he could see it now—poor-spirited and cheap against the riot of outrageous gaiety that surrounded it. He looked for datable architectural detail, but found it somehow unrecognizable in its polychrome vestments. Then the name *Potter* caught his eye from the south wall, and he walked over to it. *Sir Gerald Potter, Knight.* That was it. In Sir Gerald's time, the landlord had said. In loving memory of him, this was, in black and white marble, very expensive and in doubtful taste. Or rather—not so much in bad taste as out of period. The effect was Edwardian, even to the phrasing. He was seized with the conviction that Sir Gerald had done the drafting himself and enjoyed it. 1960. Not so long ago. And only fifty-two when he died. Still not sixty now, if he had lived. Give him twelve to fifteen years on his wife and put her in her middle forties. That would be right. "Sorrowing," it said. But that was Sir Gerald's wording. The sorrowing widow had promoted her agent and become plain Mrs. Garstin. He wondered when. Not so very long ago, because Mrs. Curtis still called her my lady. Only that might be just for the pleasure it gave her. Gave Mrs. Curtis. He could not imagine that Mrs. Garstin minded at all what anyone called her.

The western end of the nave ended in two low steps with a high pointed arch over them. From there on it was the base of the tower. This was where the ringers had worked before 1880. Now it was curtained off from the body of the church and used, he guessed, as a vestry. There was nothing in or near the chancel that would provide one. He pushed aside the heavy silk and peered in. The transition was in its way as abrupt as that between porch and nave. There was no color here at all. Everything was white. Exquisite in its order and precision, but uniformly white. There was newish woodwork everywhere. On

25

one side, by the west door of the tower, there was a cubicle which was no doubt the vestry proper, where the vicar put on whatever vestments this extraordinary setting demanded. On the other side a compartment with two curtained doors looked very much like a confessional box. All around the rest of the walls, cupboards and lockers hid neatly away the multiple requirements of choir and congregation. It was all good local joinery, lovingly executed and beautifully painted.

Above it, the wall faces, pargeted and overlaid with white emulsion, showed no traces of the strains that must, if Mr. Hardcastle was right, underlie them. If cracks had been filled, someone had made a very smooth job of it. Then, high up against the west wall, he saw what looked like a pipe or duct, white-painted like the rest, but undeniable. It ran straight across and disappeared at its two ends into the north and south walls. It could not be gas or water, and was too thick for an electric duct. Now he knew. It was solid steel. Unless he was mistaken, it would end outside the walls in two wide braces, perhaps flared crosses, or those picturesque S's which, draped charmingly on the walls of old houses, delight the connoisseur of the quaint and set the surveyor's teeth on edge. He looked up at the curtain rail above his head. It ran straight across between the springing points of the arch, elegantly white-enameled, but much too heavy, even for those heavy silk curtains.

He nodded, let the curtains fall and stepped back into the nave. The tower was corseted. The stresses that should have run to earth through the corner buttresses had overflowed and were pushing the walls outward. The vast tensile strength of steel tie-rods would contain the stresses for a long time, but at last, inevitably, the braces would go. That was the weak point, where the spread load on the braces was concentrated on the ends of the ties. The nuts, or the welding, or whatever it was that took the strain there, would sheer suddenly. The ancient

26

overstrained stonework would sag like the wall of a punctured tire. Down would come baby, cradle and all. When the wind blows, he thought, when the wind blows. He shivered suddenly, and found that the brilliantly painted church was full of darkness. It must be later than he thought.

A door he had not seen opened suddenly and an enormously tall man stepped out of the wall. He was draped from neck to foot in swinging black and looked all of eight feet high. Only his head, at the top of that huge black stalk, looked much too small for the rest of him, and his glasses seemed to cover half his face. John said, "Oh," and the vicar came down a couple of steps and stood beside him. He was still immensely tall. The glasses caught the green light from the east window and looked blankly at him, but the smile was wide.

Father Freeman said, "Good evening." He did not say "Ah," or use any of the standard parsonical frills. The voice was harsh, uncultured and completely unaffected. He wished John a good evening and meant it.

"Good evening," said John. "I'm sorry—you startled me."

"Did I? Then I'm sorry, too. The door opens very quietly. Have you been looking at the church?"

The stairway to the tower, thought John. That was it, of course. There was a hexagonal turret on the northeast corner of the tower. It went higher than the roof of the nave, but not to the existing top of the tower. There would be a spiral stair giving access, once, to the bell-chamber and the top of the tower, but now only to the bell-chamber. The new stage probably had a wooden inside stair going to the roof. The Victorians' idea of a nice top to their tower did not include a stone staircase. He said, "Well—I just wandered in, really. Nothing very systematic, I'm afraid."

The glasses looked at him blankly and the expression of the face did not change. He saw at once that flippancy would not

27

do. The man had no lightness in him. He said, "I have been looking at it, of course. But only for a minute or two. I found it startling."

The vicar nodded. "The color?" he said.

"Yes, I think so. Did you work on any particular plan?"

The vicar caught his breath, hesitated and began to walk back along the nave. Like many very tall men, he walked with a forward stoop, thrusting his small round head forward while his cassock swished to his short quick stride. He said, "I didn't do it." He seemed impatient, as if he was tired of explaining what seemed to him self-evident. "The people did it, of course. They did it as they liked. I don't think they had a plan. It's nicely done, isn't it?"

They stopped by the south door, and John looked at the bejeweled dusk round him. He wanted very much to say what he thought, but could not make up his mind what it was. "Yes," he said at last. "It's very well done indeed." He was conscious, with relief, of no hypocrisy.

"That's right. You should see it in a proper light. I must go now. There's no reason why you should. Good evening, Mr. Smith."

John said, "Good evening" to the black retreating shoulders. The great door shut heavily but quietly. He looked around once more at the dark church, shook his head and followed the vicar outside. The vicar was already through the lych gate when he came out of the porch. He hesitated, walked out through Church Lane and turned west. It would be dark soon, and he knew what Coyle was like when it was dark. He stepped out briskly, making for the bridge.

It had been difficult to judge distances in that intense darkness, and he found he had really very little idea how far it would be. There must be a ridge of some sort between the village and the river, because the road, as he had found with gratitude when

28

he had walked it the first time, ran very gently downhill from quite near the bridge to the end of the village street. Only he had not needed to use it, because someone had mended his car for him. He walked on, looking for something like a milestone that a person who liked roosting, and was not too big for it, could roost on when she was not mending cars.

The road leveled out and even, he thought, began to fall slightly; he looked ahead and saw the humped tarmac and stone parapets of the bridge. But there had been a milestone, damn it —a milestone or something of the sort. Something that would support more than a disembodied voice. He turned and went back. The car had stopped, he remembered, about twenty yards before the road began to drop toward the village. Somewhere very near here, surely. Then he saw what it was.

It was the idea of stone that had put him off. He had been looking for stones, and what he wanted was stocks. It was a tree stump, standing among the close-grown boles of living trees, but cut off short three or four feet above the ground. An ash, by the look of it. He pictured a fallen tree across the road and a hasty tidying-up job to get the road clear. The stem had been cut straight through in one piece with a chain saw, and the round top was level and reasonably smooth. He could roost on it himself if he had to. He did not at the moment see much purpose in doing so. He turned again and walked back toward the bridge.

The noise of the water was not at all loud until he was almost between the parapets. Then he saw why. The stream had cut itself a deep channel and ran between miniature cliffs of soft brown rock. The center arch of the bridge must have been all of twenty feet above the water. He heard the clack of high heels on tarmac and almost simultaneously saw a head come over the curve of the bridge ahead of him.

Cynthia Hardcastle checked visibly. He even thought for a

29

moment that she was going to turn back. But it was too late for niceties and he kept on walking toward her. She put her head up and came on, daring him to see, as he all too clearly saw, that she had been crying. They met almost on the crown of the bridge and stood facing each other, with the brown water voluble twenty feet below them.

She said, "Oh, hullo. Daddy said will you come to dinner."

Tears or no tears, he did not want to take his eyes off her face, and did not. But he saw, blurred in the background of his vision, a man's figure walking away into the dusk at the other end of the bridge.

He said, "Thank you very much. I'd love to."

CHAPTER 4

THEY CAME without speaking to the top of the rise and walked on side by side down the gentle slope to the village. She was not really, as he had at first thought, a big girl, though handsomely curved. She was at least a head shorter than he was, and walked with a quick, decisive and purely feminine step. She was mid-blonde, sad and very lovely.

Never being a man for beating about the bush, John said, "I'm sorry something's upset you. I don't suppose I can help, but let me know."

She turned her head and gave him that quick sideways flash of green that seemed already familiar. "That's all right," she said. "Thank you. Talk about something, will you? Not you. Or me."

John, who had had an unhappy apprehension that she was going to say "Tell me all about yourself," nodded appreciatively. "Right," he said. "Lady Athaliah."

"Lady—? Oh, I know. The tower. It's a book. *Frolic Wind.* Do you know it?"

"No. No, I don't think— But I feel I should. Should I?"

"Not really. It was a mild sensation when Daddy was at Oxford. A man who was up at the time wrote it."

"What about the tower, then?"

"Oh—three noble spinster sisters in a country house, and the eldest, Lady Athaliah, had a secret tower full of sex horrors. She gets struck by lightning in an ecstasy on top of the tower, and they go in and find it all. Very sensational."

"I see, yes. I think I do remember it now. But—"

"Oh, the vicar, don't you see? Bobbing about mysteriously on the battlements. You remember Daddy's theory that he didn't want to be overlooked. That's what I meant. Only I don't really think—"

"Nor do I, actually."

"Have you met him—Old Liberty?"

"Yes. Just now. In the church. He appeared suddenly out of the staircase and gave me the fright of my life. He's an odd one, all right. I wouldn't cast him for Lady Athaliah, but I wouldn't say your father was wrong, all the same."

She thought for a bit. Then she said, "I like Old Liberty. No, I don't. That's not strictly true. One doesn't like him as a person. One doesn't know him as a person. I'm not sure, as a person, he even exists. But he conveys something, or represents something —I don't know. He's like a live wire, but not the least what you mean when you say somebody's a live wire. He's nothing in himself, but when you touch him, something comes through, and you get a shock."

John said, "It's his job."

"Yes, but I've never known anyone else actually do it before. Not like that. I mean—you meet people, even some parsons, who are so good in themselves that they make you believe in something behind them. But that's an inference. The chosen vessel is so splendid that you take the contents on trust. With this man you get it direct. It doesn't stay with him at all—that's why he's so ordinary—it just comes straight through. Like a lightning conductor."

John said, "Back to Lady Athaliah. Hence the top of the tower, I suppose."

She said perfectly seriously, "I shouldn't be surprised. Sort of

32

recharging his batteries. Anyhow, in direct touch with the power supply. And he doesn't want Daddy in the way."

"Good Lord, you do surprise me. Have you tried to explain this to your father?"

"Well—no, not really. I don't think he'd take it in. The trouble with Daddy is that he's never really grown up." She said it with a sort of regretful seriousness, as though she was admitting insanity in the family. Then she turned and looked him full in the face. "I think he senses a kindred spirit in you," she said. "Only I'm not sure he's right. Anyway, be nice to him. I'm very fond of him, and he likes you."

John stopped. Having no option, Cynthia stopped too and turned to face him. He said, "I think—no, it doesn't matter. You're unhappy about somebody else, and it wouldn't do."

She looked up at him. "All the same," she said, "what do you think?"

"I think you're the most—remarkable girl I've ever met."

"Remarkable?" She turned and walked on, considering the word. Then she said, "I think I like that. It has a nice cerebral ring to it. 'And there is nothing left remarkable beneath the visiting moon.' "

John said, "I don't feel awfully cerebral."

"Never mind. I like it. That should suffice."

They walked on in silence till they were halfway along Church Lane. Then she heaved a long sigh and turned him an untroubled countenance. "And now," she said, "tell me about yourself." He told her, and was still telling her when they turned in at the white gate.

Mr. Hardcastle, with a glass in his hand, came out into the dusk to meet them. She said, "Mr. Smith has been telling me all about himself."

"Why don't you hit her?" said Mr. Hardcastle. "Have a drink."

33

"I'd like one," said John. "I shouldn't dream of it."

"No? No, you're probably right. She'd get back at you some-how, and I don't expect you want that."

"He's met the vicar," said Cynthia.

"Have you? Well, that doesn't surprise me. Where?"

"In the church."

"Ah. You've been inside, have you? No—don't tell me. You're still confused in your mind, and you might not get it right. Who else have you met?"

"I haven't met anyone. I've seen Mrs. Garstin."

"Have you? I'm glad. Else had you left unseen a wonderful piece of work which not to have been blessed withal would have discredited your travel."

"Cleopatra," said John. "Just so. Is it better to be remarkable or a wonderful piece of work?" He looked at Cynthia. She smiled at him, suddenly, dazzlingly and for the first time, so that he nearly dropped his glass.

"It's rather the family play," she said.

"Is it? I'll remember that, and come prepared with apt quota-tions and subtle references. Very ingratiating. All the same—" he turned to his host—"Mrs. Garstin is a wonderful piece of work. Even if the work must, at her age, be pretty intensive."

"Be damned to you for a callow youth," said Mr. Hardcastle. "Mary Garstin is a girl by my standards. There's not much wrong with her skin. Or her figure. And she comes from Bartondale."

"She's come a long way, then."

"Well—she was brought. Partly, anyhow. Sir Gerald Potter made a lot of money and bought a title. All right, that's the standard job, so far. But he was an interesting man, with a lot of real discernment. When he picked young Mary Whatever-she-was to share his already considerable assets and prospects, he did much more than pick a pretty face and figure to hang his money on. She's done well—really well. Manufacturing money at Upsindon mightn't have been an easy proposition at all. They bought it from the last of the Rowlands, who'd been there for generations. And I mean—this isn't the Bucks Chilterns. But it's an interesting cycle, if you're interested in social oddities. She married money and became Lady Potter. Now she's married a gentleman and become plain Mrs."

John said, "Mrs. Curtis called her 'my lady, Mrs. Garstin.' I thought myself she probably didn't mind what she was called."

"Nor does she. That wouldn't be her at all. You'll see when you meet her."

"If I meet her. She doesn't know I exist."

Cynthia said, "But you say you saw her. Where? Did she see you?"

"In the public bar at the Bell. She came in through the kitchen and appeared suddenly behind the bar."

"And she saw you?"

"Well—I was in her line of vision. She didn't register."

Cynthia sighed. "You have a lot to learn about Mrs. Garstin. She saw you all right. And you'll meet her, unless you get out pretty early tomorrow. That's up to you."

Mr. Hardcastle said, "So young and so untender."

"So young, my lord, and true." She turned to John, surveying him dispassionately. "I'll be interested to see how you make out," she said.

"I'll tell you, I promise. A round-by-round commentary. If that's what you want."

She nodded, still looking at him. "Yes," she said, "that's what I want."

"And I'm not to get out early tomorrow?"

"No. No, don't do that. I believe you might give Lady Potiphar a run for her money."

"I see. Like Joseph."

She looked at him blankly. "Joseph was her steward," she

said. "Isn't it time we ate?"

An hour later Mr. Hardcastle said, "I didn't know men of your age liked cigars. You smoke that very intelligently."

"Good God," said John, "of course we like them. We don't smoke them much because we can't afford them."

"No, I suppose not." He blew a trickle of smoke delicately through his nostrils. "It's no business of mine," he said, "but if you're not in a hurry, I hope you will stay on for a bit. I won't suggest your moving in here. You'll be better sleeping at the Bell. But eat here as often as you like, of course."

John examined the ash of his cigar thoughtfully and decided it was not yet ripe. "That's very nice of you," he said. "No, be damned to that for a social cliché. I really mean, if you'd like me to stay on for a bit, I'd very much like to."

"That's it. I should. Good." He got up and walked to the uncurtained window. "It's Cynthia," he said, "of course."

"Yes? Yes, well that doesn't surprise me. I'm not—I'm not exactly doing you a favor, you know."

"No? All right. You're old enough to decide your own terms."

John took the ash off his cigar and saw, regretfully, that it was the last one. "I'd better be going," he said. "Has Cynthia gone to bed?"

"I don't know where she is. But you won't see her again tonight."

"I see. I'll be off, then."

He came out on to the terrace and saw the tower outlined against the faint lights of Coyle. "No bells tomorrow?" he said.

"Not tomorrow. Good night."

John said, "Good night and thank you." He shut the white gate behind him and picked his way carefully down the dark steps into deeper darkness. The church was wholly dark. Nothing stirred there, but he felt, because he knew it was there, the endless, not quite static battle between the forces of gravity and the huge structure thrust up by man in their defiance. It was a long time, he thought, since man, hauling on ropes or sweating loaded up ladders, had forced these stones upward and hooked them there, one on top of the other, progressively above their proper level. Man had made a wonderful job of it, dividing the fierce opposing forces, spreading them thinly over his defenses, channeling them harmlessly down to the immutable bedrock through pier and buttress, until the whole thing was nearly, very, very nearly, static and in balance. But then man had overreached himself, and at once, insensibly but at once, the battle was no longer static and things had begun to shift. There was nothing to hear, nothing to see. But all the time, he knew, the stones were moving. He hurried on, anxious to get down into the unarguable stability of the village street.

The Bell was faintly lit, as it had been the night before, but now he did not expect the bar to be full. There was nothing of the Sabbath about Coyle's Sunday, but he reckoned it would go to bed early. He did not want to go to bed yet himself. He did not even want to pass, fresh from dining at Galehanger, between the contrary interests of Mr. and Mrs. Curtis. His cigar, as a good one should, had cleared and stimulated his mind, and he felt restless but uncertain of his direction.

He was too honest and too experienced not to know what he really wanted. He wanted to see Cynthia. She had talked little at dinner, but had watched him, with a poker face but undisguised interest, as he had talked and listened, mainly listened, to her father. He had not attempted to bring her into the conversation when she so obviously did not want to be brought. He had hoped to be able to talk to her afterward, but she had vanished without explanation or leave-taking, Mr. Hardcastle had brought out his cigars and that was how the evening had ended. And when he had asked after her, her father had said, "You won't see her again tonight." It was an odd phrase, and

37

had inevitably made it immediately plain to him that that was the one thing he wanted to do. But he did not know how to set about it. Following a mental association rather than a reasoned calculation, he turned right and walked up toward the bridge.

There was a breeze blowing, not of much strength, but enough to fill the narrow road with a continuous barrier of sound. If half the village had been weeping in the trees tonight, he would not have heard them. He would hardly have heard approaching footsteps until they were almost on him. But no one came to meet him; and when he came, full of consciously foolish expectation, to the roadside stump, no one roosted on it, and no one spoke to him out of the roadside darkness. He walked over and patted the dead wood gently, as if to propitiate whatever spirit dwelt, or had dwelt, in or on it. Then, idly now and with undisguised resignation, he walked on toward the bridge.

It was so dark, even in the comparatively clear space above the water, that he saw the figure at first only as an extension of the parapet it was sitting on. He was still not fully sure of it when it stirred and got up. It startled him, but there was no element of pleasure, even of hope, in his surprise. Whoever it was, he knew with an immediate and indefeasible conviction that it was not Cynthia.

The man said, "Oh—good evening." The noise and darkness had worked both ways, and he too had been taken by surprise. They peered at each other in the murk, each finding himself at a disadvantage and each subject to the desperate instinct of the male to pass off as ordinary what he feels to be an extraordinary occasion.

John said, "Sorry if I startled you. It's dark as the inside of a whale." He spoke as to a man of his own kind. There was no mistaking the good-evening.

The man said, "Yes, it is dark." He patted his pockets, took out a cigarette case and put a cigarette in his mouth. Then he

38

thought better of it, and put it back into the case and the case back into his pocket. John thought, "He doesn't want to strike a light." He said, "I must be getting back, or I'll be shut out. Just getting a breath of air before bed."

"Yes?" said the man. He did not say, shut out of what? "I suppose—yes, I suppose I'd better be getting back too. I don't think in fact I know what time it is."

John looked at his watch. "Getting on for eleven," he said. "If you're coming my way—"

"No. No, I'm not going your way." There was so much despair in the voice that the man became conscious of it himself and pulled himself up with an almost audible jerk. He said, "You're going back to the village, I take it?"

"That's right," said John. "I'm staying at the Bell." He had the strongest possible conviction that the other man knew this perfectly well, and that they were both making conversation in a desperate effort to disengage bloodlessly from an unwanted encounter. He had an irresponsible urge to say, "I'm John Smith" and thrust out an eager hand through the intervening darkness. But he did not feel amusing, and on consideration he found that he shrank from any closer contact with the looming sorrow opposite him. He waited, while the stream rushed under the bridge and the wind moved in the trees, in the hope that the other man would think up some successful gambit of disengagement. Even as he waited, he saw that the necessary resolution was not there. It was for him to leave the man. He could not hope to be left. He thought, "Hell, this is ridiculous." He said, "Ah well . . . ," swung on his heel and started walking briskly back the way he had come. From a safe distance he called "Good night" back over his shoulder, and heard, already muted in the surrounding noise, the other man's response.

The front door of the Bell was locked. Guided by experience, he tried the door that opened into the side yard. George Curtis, blinking, made little effort to pretend that he had not been waiting up for him. Mrs. Curtis, he was glad to see, seemed to have gone to bed. He shaped himself to apologize and then thought, "It's only eleven, damn it. Why should I?"

The landlord said, "Been up at Mr. Hardcastle's?" He seemed quite cheerful about it.

"Yes," said John. "We got talking. You know what it is."

"Oh, I know what it is." He poured an immense and sinister significance into words which, as John had used them, had been almost completely meaningless.

"He's at it again," thought John. One of these days he would find a phrase, even a whole sentence, which neither of the Curtises could transfigure in this way. But not tonight. Tonight he had had enough. He said, "Good night, Mr. Curtis," and then, weakening, "Sorry to have kept you."

The landlord said, "That's all right. I'm in no hurry," and John was aware of an almost palpable suggestion of Mrs. Curtis lying unsought upstairs. He remembered the man on the bridge, stuck there, unable to move, saying, "I suppose I'd better be getting back too." No one wanted to go home tonight, he thought. No one was ready for bed. He grunted and found his way to his room.

CHAPTER 5

THE WALL began on his left almost as soon as he was over the bridge. It was an old wall built of the local stone, but for long stretches repointed and in two places completely rebuilt. An old wall reinforced with new money. It was too high to see over, but there were trees behind it. Upsindon, that came all the way down to the river on this side. He wondered what the house was like. But it would not, for certain, be very near the road.

He came to the gates a good three quarters of a mile on. The lodge had been added to, firmly, but with reasonable tact. He imagined a new kitchen and bathroom with an extra bedroom over. He was almost past when he saw, out of the corner of his eye, a flourish of stone chimneys among the background trees. Curiosity got the better of him, and he pulled the car on to the grass verge under the wall. He walked back, hoping nothing would come along the road to shame him.

The gates were new and very plain. They would shut the drive effectively, but no one had been allowed to have fun with them. The more he saw of Sir Gerald Potter, the more he liked him. There was the house now. Stuart, from what he could see, and not too big. There was a swathe of park a couple of hundred yards deep in front of it. Beyond that the land was all in hand.

There was a car coming from the direction of Coyle. It was no use pretending he was not rubber-necking. He turned his back to the road and stood squarely by the gatepost, looking up the drive toward the house. The one thing he was unprepared for was to be taken from the rear. When the car swung in and braked behind him, he turned with something of the deliberate bravado of a man facing a firing squad. At least it could not, from the sound, be the dark-blue monster with the chauffeur.

It was small, black and open. Mrs. Garstin was at the wheel. She had a scarf tied over her head and was alone. She sat there, with her hands on the wheel, looking up at him. She looked at him, giving nothing away, for so long that he had time to appraise, not so much her, as the effect she had on him. It was, he thought, her complete assurance that gave her this power. Or perhaps the power had given her the assurance. All he knew was that the power and the assurance were there, involving him in a single experience. Then she leaned forward, switched off the engine and smiled.

He smiled himself, looking down at her, reflecting like a mirror the warmth she threw up at him. That was really, he thought, the essence of the matter. You did not deal with this woman; you simply reacted to her. He did not know how clever she might be in calculating and getting the reaction she wanted in any particular case. He doubted if there was much calculation in her. It was not her mind, or even her personality, that affected you. She was there as a phenomenon, a wonderful piece of work, as Mr. Hardcastle had said, an anthropomorphic projection of natural forces. Aphrodite of Upsindon.

She said, "Do you want to see the house?" Her voice went with the rest of her. It was an unconscious emanation of her physical presence, not something she consciously used.

He nodded, still smiling. "I got a glimpse of it as I went past," he said. "I wanted to have a better look. I knew it was yours, of course."

She leaned across and opened the near-side door. "Get in,"

42

she said. She turned, restarted the engine and put the car in gear. She did not wait to see what he would do or watch him as he got in. She simply waited until he had shut the door and then let in the clutch. She drove, as she did everything, with a sort of placid confidence, and he looked at her sideways as she drove. She was not, he decided, a beauty. She was, in her way, quite perfect, but you did not judge her aesthetically.

The house was brick with dressings of what looked like Bath stone, topped out with the clustered chimneys which had caught his eye. Mrs. Garstin got out and went straight up the formal steps between the knopped balustrades, leaving him to follow her. Every movement was rounded and unhurried. It was for the world to hurry, if it must, as it revolved about her. She was at the point of rest. In the hall she turned and said, "You like houses? Go anywhere you want. Then come and have coffee—in there." She pointed and left him. He watched her helplessly until the door closed behind her. Then he turned and wandered up the great oak stairs.

He came out into a paneled gallery, ghost-marked with the Rowland portraits which Sir Gerald, with his sure touch, had refused to take over. Halfway along it a door opened, and a man came out and turned in John's direction. He had one of those lean, bony faces that mature at eighteen and change little. He might have been anywhere near thirty, but the eyes, deep-set and piercing, did not look young. He bowed gravely to John and John, full of a sort of vicarious assurance, bowed back.

The man said, "You're Mr. Smith, I think? My name's Garstin."

John knew him at once for the night loiterer on the bridge. He knew that Mr. Garstin knew this, but it was unthinkable that either should acknowledge it. He said, "Yes, that's right." He did not for a moment feel that he was in the presence of his host. They were both, and to almost the same degree, there by invitation, even perhaps under the same constraint.

"Seeing the house?" said Mr. Garstin. He went on along the gallery and down the stairs.

John said, "Yes," again. He said it casually, after they had already passed, hardly noticing the oddity of the encounter.

It was the boy who really surprised him. John came suddenly face to face with him where the gallery ended and stood there, staring into the rather insolent blue eyes under the thatch of unkempt yellow hair. It was only later that he remembered the small, delicately modeled mouth and chin that were the mother's contribution. He could not say why, but the fairness shocked him. He had not pictured Sir Gerald as fair. The boy said, "Hullo? My mother ask you in? I'm Derek Potter." He wore a sweater and jeans. John wondered whether he should, in the modern classification, be called a student or a teen-ager. Student, he decided. Probably Redbrick. He said, "Yes. John Smith."

The boy nodded and smiled, not at John, but at something in his own mind. John did not take to him. Derek said, "You don't live in these parts, do you?"

John said, "No. I'm staying in Coyle for a bit."

"Aha. Not been there long, though?"

A number of fairly crude retorts rose to his tongue, but he held them in check. He smiled genially into the insolent, wary eyes and said, "No."

The boy too was clever enough not to pursue the implications. He contented himself with smiling, as he had before, at what he knew they were both thinking. He said, "Have you seen my step-daddy?"

John said, "Yes, he's just gone downstairs." He sidestepped and walked past Derek Potter, leaving him standing there. Whether or not the boy had any other lines of attack in mind, he did not try them on a vanishing opponent. For a moment he hesitated, and John imagined a slightly disconcerted defiance wasted on the timeless air of the paneled gallery. Then he walked on and went down the stairs.

John, still armed with a curious dreamlike assurance, pursued his exploration of the house. All the inhabitants he knew of were, after all, to his knowledge downstairs. There must be servants, but at this time of the morning they would be downstairs too. In any case he had authority to go wherever he wanted. The scented air, even as he opened the door, told him that this was Mrs. Garstin's bedroom. He went in and shut the door behind him. He looked at the few, austere bottles on the dressing table, and remembered guiltily what he had said to Mr. Hardcastle about intensive work. Not wholly a stranger to the bedrooms of much younger women, he had never seen less clutter. Not but what one of Mrs. Garstin's few bottles could probably, he thought, buy out the massed experiments of artless and unmarried youth. There was no ornament anywhere. No picture on the walls, no frills on the drapes, nothing that did not have its proper work to do. Not even, he realized, any books. Whatever Mrs. Garstin did in bed, she did not read. The bed, plain, vast and no doubt technically perfect, dominated the room. Everything else was muted and shut away behind flush doors or in drawers with recessed handles. The peace of mind that flowed from her as palpably as the scent she used, and was inextricably blended with it, filled the air and held his perceptive senses in check. There was no second bed.

He did not expect her to ask him what he thought of the house, and she did not. She was there, sitting back in a rather deep and masculine armchair, with the coffee tray at her side, watching the door as he came in. She said, "That's right," and leaned forward to pour out the coffee. There were only two cups on the tray. He sat in the obvious chair, close to her, but facing

45

her and sitting higher, and looked at her as she handled the things. He thought he could be content, almost, to watch her forever, moving and doing things, if she would only let him stay within sight of her.

She handed him his coffee and said, "Why did you come to Coyle?"

"I didn't really. I was passing through. But I had a stoppage with the car and decided to stay the night. Then Mr. Hardcastle asked me to breakfast, and I decided to stay on for a bit. There's nothing else much I ought to be doing at the moment."

She thought about this. He thought about it himself, wondering how far it was reasonably accurate and complete. Then she said, "You like Mr. Hardcastle?"

"I like him very much," he said, and she wrinkled her brow and looked at him, in some way at a loss for the first time in his acquaintance with her. She said, "He's a funny man. Cynthia's lovely. And of course she's cleverer than her father." She did not invite his opinion on any of these points, and he volunteered none.

After a bit she said, "My husband likes Mr. Hardcastle. I don't think Derek does. I don't think Derek likes anyone much."

"He's not keen on me," said John.

She never took her eyes off him, nor he off her. She was a person, he saw now, to whom words meant little or nothing. Words, which to people like him and the Hardcastles were more real than reality, and had an independent validity, to her were as artificial and unsatisfactory as a papier-mâché mask. He knew her, already, very, very much better than he had when she had stopped and taken him into her car. But not because of anything either of them had said. If anything, in spite of it. There was an immediate interchange of consciousness, as there is be-

46

tween lovers, though they had not so much as touched hands.
All day the same our postures were, and we said nothing all the
day. Words were a weariness and a burden.

They drank another cup of coffee each, and then she stood up
out of her deep armchair, very slowly and with the same in-
evitability of movement, and he went straight up to her and
took hold of both her hands. He thought quite clearly, as he did
so, that he had no idea what might happen next; but to touch
her and take her hands seemed the obvious necessity. He heard
someone moving in the hall for quite a while before he let go
of her hands. He moved away from her only as the door opened.
So far as he remembered afterward, she had not moved at all
throughout; only her hands had been there, ready to be taken
hold of, when he had gone up to her.

Old Liberty's head ducked under the high oak lintel of the
door frame and seemed almost to be looking at them from over
the top of the half-opened door. Then the whole man was with
them, following the small, thrust-forward head across the room.

Father Freeman did not appear to have seen John at all. He
walked straight past him to Mrs. Garstin and took both her hands
in his. She still did not seem to have moved, except that her
eyes were turned up to meet those of a man a good head taller.
John had a lunatic conviction that someone else ought to come
in next and take her hands from those of Father Freeman, but
he could not think who it could be. Not, he felt sure, Mr. Garstin. The vicar said, "Mary," in his harsh voice, and John saw at
once that this time it was Mrs. Garstin who was on the receiving
end. Whatever power she possessed, this gangling man was im-
pervious to it. Instead, the vicar put all his power, whatever it
was and wherever he got it from, into the clasp of his bony hands
and the downward stare of his small spectacled eyes. It was difficult to see what she felt about it, except that she seemed content
to leave things as they were. She made no attempt to take her

47

hands or her eyes from his.

"Mary," said the vicar, "I've been wanting to talk to you about the festival. It's on the tenth, as you know. You will be there?"

She said, "Oh yes, I'll be there." She still did not move.

Father Freeman smiled suddenly. It transfigured his whole face as if it was galvanized from inside, but Mrs. Garstin did not smile back. It was as though they were in contact only through the eyes, and the smile had not got that far. He said, "Good. Good. You know how much I am relying on you. How much we all are."

Quite suddenly John knew what it was all about. There was one possible source, Mr. Hardcastle had said, but Old Liberty had not succeeded in tapping it yet. Twenty thousand pounds, or as much of it as remained uncollected. Most of it, almost certainly. He tried to reconcile his confused but overwhelming impression of Mrs. Garstin with the giving of twenty thousand pounds to prop up a falling church tower, but could make nothing of it.

The vicar suddenly let go of Mrs. Garstin's hands and moved slightly back from her. His eyes came around and met John's for a moment, but they had nothing in them. She said, "Do you know Mr. Smith? He's staying in Coyle."

The vicar nodded without turning his head. He was looking at Mrs. Garstin again. "Yes," he said, "we've already met." He caught his breath as if he was about to say something, but thought better of it. He stood for a moment with his head bowed, not looking at either of them. It was as if he was listening to something neither of them could hear. Whatever it was, it had his undivided attention. Then he suddenly looked up and spoke to Mrs. Garstin again. "I'll write to you," he said. "But I had to see you. I had to be sure." He caught his breath again and let it go in a long sigh. "I had to come," he said again. Then he turned with a swish of cassock skirts and made for the door. He opened it and stood for a moment with his hand on the handle. He looked at John as if he was seeing him for the first time and then again at Mrs. Garstin. Then he nodded and went out, shutting the door after him.

She was standing now, as John turned back to her, by the cold coffee cups, staring at the door. Her hands were behind her back. She turned to him as he moved, but her eyes were hardly with him. She said, "You'd better go now."

He said, "Yes, I will. Thank you for—" He made a rather helpless gesture and said, "Thank you for letting me see the house. And for the coffee."

"I'm glad you came," she said. She said it as if she meant it, but all the world was between them.

John said, "Goodbye, then." He went out into the hall, not pausing to look back. Derek Potter was standing at the top of the steps. A small car, which John took to be the vicar's, was turning out of the gates on the road. Derek said, "You going too? Old Liberty seems to have broken up the session."

"He came on business, I think."

"Oh, he came on business, all right. Never relaxes, Old Liberty. Curious type, don't you think?"

John, considering the matter, saw no reason to disagree. "Yes," he said, "I think he is. Is he nice to you?"

The question, as he had hoped, was unexpected and caught the boy off balance. "Nice to me?" he said. "I don't know. I don't think so, particularly. I mean—I'm never quite sure he knows I exist. It's a bit disconcerting, in fact."

"Yes, indeed. I know exactly what you mean. Very disconcerting indeed."

Derek, puzzled by an unlooked-for lack of opposition, suddenly lowered his guard. He smiled at John. It remained a rather provocative smile, but there was a whiff of genuine feeling in it. He said, "I know what he's after."

John said, "Will he get it?"

Derek was no longer smiling. "Over my dead body," he said.

John nodded and set out for his car.

CHAPTER 6

"St. Udan," said Mr. Hardcastle, "was an almost totally obscure saint and martyr. If you are one of the pagan school, you can identify him, rather obviously I cannot help thinking, with a local wood god. The guardian spirit of the Gale, I suppose. It is easier to say that he was a Christian centurion who suffered under the persecution of Domitian. If the records are to believed, Domitian practically decimated the legions." He drank his coffee to the bottom and pushed his cup away. "Personally," he said, "I identify him privately with that youthful martyr Gibbon speaks of, who was tied down on a bed of roses and set upon, presumably before an appreciative audience, by a beautiful and lascivious courtesan. Do you remember? Finding himself unable to control his rising passion, he bit off his own tongue. I have never been able to make out why he did not bite the beautiful courtesan. She must have been within range and asking for it. It's true Gibbon does not say he died, but loss of blood, or septicemia, or possibly suffocation on the spot—very likely if he was tied on his back, as he presumably was . . . Anyway, he was remembered in the church. Of course, we don't know his name. But then with St. Udan that's all we do know, so it seems a pity not to put the two together. But I haven't tried this on Father Freeman."

John said, "Tell me about this festival. I heard the vicar mention it."

"Well, I don't know much myself. I'm in the wrong camp, you see. They probably think I'd wish foul weather on them or something. But I think it's simply a grand celebration of the saint's day. St. Udan hasn't, I think I'm right in saying, got an official day in the church's calendar, but there's always been a bonfire here on the tenth. I know there's to be a procession of some sort. It's money, of course, he's after. Well—no, that's a bit unjust. He wants to tie up the saint's day with a recognized occasion for local junketing. And he will, you'll see. I told you it's all pure medieval. But he won't miss the occasion to raise money for his fund. You can be sure of that."

"This procession—"

"Oh, the choir, and the various bodies with their banners, and the children—you can imagine. It will be very well done. We haven't got a band, but they sing like anything. What they ought to have, of course, is *tableaux vivants* on farm wagons— well, tractors and trailers, perhaps, now—with scenes from the life of the saint. That would be the real thing. Especially if they would accept my theory of the martyrdom. The casting should present no problems. And people love dressing up. And undressing, for the matter of that. Look how many times a year Godiva rides anywhere within fifty miles of Coventry."

John said, "Mrs. Garstin has promised to be present. I wondered—"

"She has, has she? Not, presumably, in a dramatic role?"

"No. But—you said the vicar hadn't yet succeeded in tapping one possible source of the money he wants. I wondered if she was it."

Mr. Hardcastle narrowed his eyes and looked at John. So, thought John, he must, when he was a junior don, have looked at one of his duller undergraduates who had scored an unexpected bull-point in an otherwise innocent essay. He said, "What makes you think that?"

52

John said, "Only the way he talked to her. That, I suppose, and the fact that she presumably has the money."

"You interest me, I must say. When was this?"

"Yesterday. I think all he actually said was that she must be there for the festival because they were all relying on her. But the implications seemed to me to be considerable. And something had obviously been said before. He came just to keep the pressure up."

"This was at Upsindon?"

"Yes."

Mr. Hardcastle allowed himself the slightest nod. John said, "I went to see the house and was given coffee." Mr. Hardcastle made a quick, deprecating movement of his hand, as if to disclaim any intention of asking for an explanation. "Oh," said John, "and there was something Derek Potter said. He takes the same view, unless I'm mistaken."

"Indeed, indeed? I don't imagine our Derek would approve?"

"No. Can she—I mean, could she in fact afford it?"

"I don't know, of course. But I mean—she's not the Ford Foundation or the Gulbenkian Trust. Can any ordinary person afford twenty thousand these days? I shouldn't have thought so. I don't think Sir Gerald was a millionaire. Just a standard tycoon."

"What puzzles me—I mean if there really is any question of her finding the whole lump—is why she should want to."

"Ah." Mr. Hardcastle pushed his chair back and felt for his pipe. "That, I agree, is where the interest lies. Not whether she can, or even whether she will, but why she should." He wandered out on to the terrace, filling his pipe as he went. John, who amused himself by the ease with which he slipped into the role of attentive disciple, wandered cheerfully after him. They sat side-saddle on the stone coping, puffing smoke quietly at the morning panorama of Coyle. "I don't know what you think," said Mr. Hardcastle, "but I have an idea it would be something to do with the command of allegiance."

John frowned at him. "Whose command of whose allegiance?"

"Her command of his—Old Liberty's. She commands all our allegiances, after all. Mine, certainly. Yours, I imagine." He repeated the small deprecating gesture. "But Old Liberty's sterner stuff. He is for God the Father, not the mother goddess. I wonder—I only wonder, mark you, I don't know—but I wonder whether the command of allegiance might not become an addiction. A habit of command that will allow no exceptions. Other sorts of power do it. Well, it's a commonplace. And after all, they're both here for keeps. She's the lady of Upsindon and he's vicar of Coyle. The relation, whatever it is, is a permanent one. There is no dodging it. Do you see what I mean? But it's pure speculation, I admit. I don't even know the suggestion is there. Though your independent evidence weighs with me, I must say."

John puffed for a minute in silence, wrinkling his brow. Then he said, "I must admit, the idea did occur to me, watching them both, that in some sense Mrs. Garstin had met her match, and was a bit out of her depth. But I thought of it more as a direct bringing to bear of influence—on his part, I mean. You put a rather more subtle aspect on it."

Mr. Hardcastle did not take this amiss. "Speculation," he said, "only speculation. But enjoyable. What did you make of Derek?"

"I didn't take to him at first, to be honest. But once I'd disarmed his antagonism, I thought I caught a glimpse of something not necessarily unlikable."

"He's got brains. That's his trouble. His father had, of course. He's a lot cleverer than his mother."

For a moment John groped in his mind. Then he remembered

where he had heard the formula before. He smiled, but very privately. He said, "What does he do?"

"Derek? He's at Bartondale. Reading chemistry. Not a case of using Dad's name, I assure you, though they were probably glad to get a Potter. He could have got in anywhere, I imagine. But he chose Bartondale. I think it was a gesture. Rather a gallant one. He'd have been—what?—fourteen or so when his father died. And the present position can't be easy. There's nothing of the young squire about Derek."

"No, that there certainly isn't. How does he get on with Garstin?" My step-daddy, he thought, touched with a sudden wave of compassion for the insolent, antagonistic Derek.

"I think in fact not badly, as person to person. It's the position he dislikes. And he must, I suppose, involve Garstin to some extent in the wrongness of the position. But I believe as a person he's sorry for him, as much as anything. He's not the only one, of course."

John said, "I know that," and Cynthia came out on to the terrace, breathtaking in the yellow morning sunshine. She said, "Good morning, Daddy," and gave John a friendly nod.

"Good morning, Cynthia. Have you had your breakfast?"

"Yes, yes. Earlier. I'm going into Frantham. Any commissions?"

"I don't think so. Oh yes, tobacco. The usual."

She looked at John. Suddenly bold, he said, "Would you like me to drive you in? I still haven't seen Frantham."

She gave him the quick, appraising glance she had borrowed from her father. Then she said, "Yes, if we can have the car open. Ours doesn't."

"We can and will. You can even drive if you like. It will be an experience for you."

Mr. Hardcastle got up from the wall. "If Cynthia drives," he said, "it will be an experience for both of you. I wish you joy of it." He vanished into the house.

Cynthia said, "Give me a minute to fix my motoring veil." She, too, vanished, and John, apprehensive but exultant, knocked out his pipe and prepared himself for whatever was to come.

She emerged a minute later in a leather jerkin with a scarf knotted uncompromisingly under her chin. She said, "Where is she? At the Bell?"

"Yes. Where does yours live, by the way? It never occurred to me. Or do you drive it up and down the steps?"

"There's a road at the back. Through the wood. But it's a bit of a way round."

John opened the gate for her, and they went down the steps together. He said, "Do you mend cars often?"

"Not for choice. Only when I can't keep my hands off them."

"Or when you have reasons of your own for wanting them mobile?"

She suddenly put out a hand and gave his hand a small quick squeeze. "I'm sorry," she said.

John kept his eyes resolutely ahead. Apart from other considerations, he wanted if possible to avoid falling headlong down the steps. He said, "You needn't be sorry. But it was a miscalculation. At least, staying to tell me was."

"Only partly. I wanted—I thought you were worth having a second look at. But in any case—I mean, you'd only have pushed her into Coyle. Flesh and blood couldn't bear it. If you'd got a dead car working by flashlight inside two minutes, could you bear to see the owner push it off, not knowing what you'd done? Be fair."

"If I'd done anything remotely approaching it, I'd tell everybody I met for the next three days. But I can't really imagine its happening. Where did you acquire this unfeminine facility?"

"Books," she said. "And mucking about. George tinkers cars

56

and used to let me help him."

"George?"

"George Curtis."

"Ah. A fellow member of the opposition. Yes, I see."

"I'm only an honorary member. I even go to church sometimes. Go to Evensong on Sunday. It's an experience."

He nodded, and they turned into Church Lane. The car stood
in the Bell yard. He folded the hood back, and she got into the
driving seat. George Curtis came out of the side door and said
to her, "You'll have to watch the steering. Get her too far to the
right and she won't come back. Not without you give her a
good wrench." He looked at her gloomily. "It's the track rod,"
he said. "Worn terrible." John stood there with his hand still on
the folded hood, looking from one to the other of them. He
felt the shamed helplessness of the accused's parent in a ju-
venile court. He wanted to protest that he loved his car and
had always done everything for it. Cynthia nodded, reached
with unerring certainty for the proper controls and started the
engine. It roared with a full-throated splendor that John found
immensely comforting. Cynthia and George Curtis drooped
their heads sideways, like thrushes over a worm-filled lawn, listening for he knew not what. Then they straightened up and
exchanged significant nods. Cynthia said to John, "Are you getting in?" She spoke very kindly.

"If you think it will be all right. Are you capable of giving her
a good wrench if you get too far to the right and she won't come
back?"

"I expect so." He got into the unfamiliar passenger seat and
shut himself in. She said, "I'm not a very good driver, in fact."

"You are—I mean, you have got a license?"

"Oh yes. I passed the test." She let in the clutch and the car
moved unsteadily backward. "Eventually," she said. She got
into first and took a run at the gate of the yard. George Curtis,

57

John noticed, had already stepped well back into the doorway. She turned and waved to him. " 'Bye, George," she shouted, and so, with her head still over her shoulder, moved out into the street. There was, as she had assumed, nothing coming from either direction. She changed her gears faultlessly, took three successive corners on the plumb crown of the road and set course, still in the middle of the road, for Frantham, twenty miles away.

The Antelope was picturesque and centrally placed. It was also, apparently, the only thing of its kind in Frantham. "Why only two stars?" said John. "I was going there when I was diverted to the Bell. I pictured something much scruffier."

"Did you want something scruffy?"

"I wanted something cheap. As it is, I pay the Curtises next to nothing for my room and do most of my eating at Galehanger. Do you mind?"

"No. The Antelope won't get more than two stars until they do something about the plumbing. But the food's all right."

"Do they make coffee? I need some, I think."

They were drawn into the curb opposite the hotel. She eased her scarf back off the top of her head and turned and looked at him. "Cold?" she said.

"Scared mostly. I'm sorry. At least I didn't scream. I know James Bond's girls all drive sports cars at over ninety, but they're all rally-class drivers. It's one of the essential qualifications."

She sniffed. "I don't think they could mend them. But then they never go wrong."

"You're perfectly right. I'm not really being mean. I'm just not James Bond."

"No? Well, that's something, anyway. The Antelope's coffee is nice, as it happens. Let's have some."

Over the coffee she said, "Tell me about Round One."

58

"Round One?"

"You promised me a round-by-round commentary."

"Oh Lord, so I did. That was before I'd met her."

"You'd seen her. Wasn't that enough? She's a most triumphant lady, if report be square to her."

"Ah, but she wasn't in a barge with silken tackle and all the rest. She was in a sports car. Almost James Bond class, now I come to think of it."

"And she can drive. I know. Go on."

He gazed unhappily into his coffee cup. He said, "Nothing happened. That's the odd thing. We drank coffee. We spoke trivialities. I touched her hand once. Then the vicar came in."

"Ah. Cleopatra again. The holy priests bless her—"

"No," he said. "No, I don't think so."

She stared at him with rather baleful green eyes. "Riggish," she said. "What a word. No?"

"No. At least, I think Old Liberty's blessing would be strictly conditional. She'd have to earn it."

"Well, that's something, too. How?"

"Money. Quite a lot of money, I reckon."

She put her cup down with a bang. She said, "You don't mean the tower?"

"I don't know, of course. But—yes, for what it's worth, that's my guess."

"But—why?"

"That's what your father said. Why?"

She said, "I'd like to think about that." She stood up. "Now we'd better shop. I like shopping alone. Do you mind?"

"No. So do I, as a matter of fact. How long do you want?"

"Half an hour. There's not much. Meet you at the car."

"Right." She went, and he called, still rather unhappily, for the bill.

She returned to the car, he noticed, exactly on time. "You

drive," she said.

"Not if you're just humoring me."

"No, no. I want to relax." They got in and set off sedately through the small-town traffic. They were just clear of the houses, and beginning to pick up speed, when a small black saloon cut in between them and the van ahead, waited a moment for the oncoming car and was off again before he had time, or felt the need, to check his speed for it. He had a glimpse of a very pale intent face and a pile of dark hair. He nodded. "Neat," he said. "A bit ruthless, but neat."

She was looking straight ahead and did not turn her head. "Sheila," she said. "Neat but ruthless, you think?"

"I said ruthless but neat. But I meant the driving, of course. Sheila who?"

"Drew. Sheila Drew. She works in the estate office."

"Upsindon?"

"Yes." She invited no further questions and he asked none. They drove in silence through the golden air, and when he swung the car through the archway into the yard of the Bell, she turned and smiled at him, and the day seemed safe again. She said, "I really did enjoy that. I hope I didn't spoil it for you."

"It was yours to spoil if you wanted to. But you didn't, no."

"Mine to spoil?"

"Yours to make and to unmake. It wasn't Frantham I went to see. Or the Antelope. Do you mind?"

She got out and gathered her parcels from behind the seat while he sat still at the wheel, unwilling to move till she answered. She walked around to his side of the car and stood there, looking down at him. "I didn't really suppose it was," she said. "No, I don't think I mind at all. Only—" She frowned, feeling for the words she wanted. "Only take it slow, won't you? There's a good deal on the road, and I don't think I'm fully insured."

60

He nodded, and she went, carrying her parcels, out through the archway into the street. He eased himself out of the seat and went into the bar. "Beer," he said to George Curtis.

"That's as you like. I'd say gin."

John shrugged. "You know best," he said. The landlord gave him gin.

CHAPTER 7

THE WIND got up late in the afternoon. It rolled a blanket of dark cloud across the rim of the valley, so low that it seemed to sweep the top of the banked trees. The blanket moved continuously, but did not lift. Coyle, after its short swim in sunlight, settled back into its proper dark.

George Curtis's gin, welcome at the time, had been a mistake, but it was too late to rectify it now. Exercise, John knew, was the only remedy, but a familiar lethargy held him back. He went out into the village street and looked about him, but saw no solution either way. He walked down Church Lane, elaborately uncommitted until he reached the lych gate. Then he refused, by a last conscious effort of will, the flagged path to his left and went in through the gate.

The gusts funneled themselves in the valley, rolling in visible waves along the trees of the Gale and moaning in the superfluous crenelations at the top of the tower. He almost expected to see the tower itself move as the trees moved, but it stood up with the impolitic obstinacy of the oak, which will strip itself in a gale when lesser trees bow and save themselves. But he did not think the tower would fall today. He went into the church, shut the door quietly behind him and went straight to the door in the wall that gave on to the stair. He half expected, after all that had been said, to find it locked, but knew that was not in character. The whole church lay open.

62

The smell of old stone was very strong in the dark tube and there were voices everywhere. He went steadily up, walking on the worn treads at the outer edges of the stairs. The door into the ringers' chamber, where once the bells had hung, was open. Humanity met him suddenly in the narrow doorway. He even smelled humanity. There were old jackets hung on pegs, benches marked with sweat, and assorted beer mugs in a box, neatly washed and turned upside down with a tea cloth over them. It was like the changing room of a local cricket club. There were graffiti on the whitewashed walls, but insignificant and certainly innocent. There was no record board to perpetuate past feats. That was, perhaps, for amateurs. These people rang for their lives. He got no farther than the threshold, leaning in and looking around. Whatever he was looking for, it was not here. He drew back and went on up the stair.

The next door was shut. He put a hand on the handle, hesitated and then turned it and pushed. The drop latch clanked up in its cage and the door swung heavily. He expected to be frightened and was. He had been in bell-chambers before. There was always something frightening in the gaping upturned mouths of the balanced monsters, ready to swing over at a touch with a ponderous rush of clanging metal. Ancient machinery, he thought, disguised much less than modern the crude strength of the forces it controlled. He went in, but could not bring himself to shut the door behind him. As he had suspected, a wooden stair, hardly more than a ladder with flat treads and a handrail, went diagonally up the smooth face of the near wall to a door at the top. He tiptoed over a yard of slatted catwalk and began to climb. The bells were below him now, gaping up at him in the gloom like a nestful of monstrous fledglings waiting to be fed. He turned his back on them and tried the door at the top of the wall. It did not move.

He pushed, and for a moment unbalanced himself on the nar-

63

row step, so that he thought he was going to fall. He clutched the handrail and steadied himself. His palm, when he relaxed his grip, was sticky on the smooth wood. The wind breathed harshly in the stone louvers, and from somewhere above him there was a steady tapping he could not identify. It was very dark.

He tried the door again, leaning his weight carefully against it as he pushed. It did not yield at all, and he saw, almost at the same instant, the heavy box lock that held it and the key hung on a nail beside it. The key turned smoothly, and this time, when he pushed, the door went back against the elastic resistance of the gusty air outside. Light and noise leaped on him as he forced the door back, and he stepped out into a gray, unfamiliar world at the top of the tower.

All around him the carefully carved turrets and battlements, hardly weathered in a hundred years, stood up and roared in the wind. The roof under his feet was leaded and slippery. The tapping he had heard from inside was loud and insistent here, and he recognized it before he turned to see the halyard beating itself phrenetically against the flagpole stepped in a corner of the wall. He let the wind shut the door behind him. There was no fastening on this side. He stepped gingerly to the nearest gap in the stonework and leaned on it, looking out and down.

Only to the north, where the trees of the Gale waved against the moving sky, was anything close above him. Everything else was at his feet, the village, the river, the road running west toward Upsindon and east toward Frantham. But farther back, whichever way he looked, the hills, mostly wooded, stood up and shut him in. He had not known, until he had climbed to its highest vantage point, how deep Coyle lay. There were lights in the village now, and Galehanger, away across the dark gap of moving air and only a little below him, shone like a ship in a line of light against its background of dusky moving trees. He

64

drifted around from gap to gap, buffeted by the damp wind and still full of an intolerable oppression that took away his power of decision but would not let him rest.

It was all but fully dark when he turned to go down. The figure facing him was black and immensely tall. Its skirts flapped about it as the halyard flapped on the tall white pole. Father Freeman came slowly across the leaded roof toward him, his hands limp at his sides, his head slightly forward, looking at him in the noisy darkness. John was conscious, not of fear, but of a weakness of spirit that cried to be delivered from whatever power it was that was coming to meet him.

When he was no more than a yard or two from him, the vicar stopped and said, "What brought you up here, Mr. Smith?"

John, his back against the cold stone and his hands half raised in front of him, looked up into the small spectacled face and shook his head. "I don't know," he said.

"The wind is getting up," the vicar said, "but the tower will not fall tonight."

John nodded, lowering his hands. "I know," he said.

"I don't think you know very much. You are one of the clever ones who know so little. Why does it interest you? What business is it of yours?"

Something in John woke and rebelled against the bitterness in the unlovely voice. The man is ignorant, he said to himself, and therefore imputes ignorance. He said, "It is no business of mine. But I think you are wrong."

"Wrong?" said the vicar. He leaned forward and peered downward at the white face pressed against the battlements of the tower. The stridency was gone, and the word was spoken quietly. It sounded hardly more than a whisper in the roaring of the wind between them.

"Wrong in what you are doing and what you are trying to do." Conviction dawned on him suddenly, and he thrust him-

65

self forward away from the stone until their faces almost touched. What he remembered, up there in the noisy darkness, was Derek Potter's disillusioned stare and the snarl in the boy's voice. Over my dead body, he had said. Dance over my lady Lee, thought John. London Bridge is falling down, and there is a time-honored way of underpinning a tottering structure. Over my dead body, Father Freeman.

The vicar's face went up and away from him. It was smiling, and John saw for himself, what he had guessed before, that the smile did not reach the eyes. Father Freeman said, "Mr. Smith, I came up here to pray. Will you leave me now?"

An immense longing to get down off the tower overwhelmed John, and he nodded but did not move. The vicar said, "I believe in your own way you want the truth. One of these days it will find you." He stood aside and pulled open the turret door against the force of the wind. He said, "It is a terrible thing, Mr. Smith, to fall into the hands of the living God. Remember that."

John nodded again and ducked into the doorway. The door slammed shut behind him, and he was alone in an immense and whispering darkness, with the balanced bells gaping below. He groped for the handrail, found it and began to go step by step down the wooden stair. On the worn stone he went faster, feeling with his left hand along the winding wall that shut him in. The ringers' chamber passed him in a gleam of dim light and the smell of old sweat. His groping hands found the bottom door and pushed at it fiercely. It did not move. He fumbled, almost desperately, for the handle, found it and stepped out into the lesser darkness on the solid floor of the nave.

He tiptoed across the flagstones, pulled the great south door inward and heard the voice of the wind waiting for him outside. But the wind was less here, and common sense reasserted itself. The gusty air poured itself down the valley, but this was not the gale that would bring the great stones down on his head. The tower would not fall tonight.

Above him, as he hesitated at the lych gate, the warm lights of Galehanger stretched along the side of the hill, split vertically by the dark column of the tower. He wanted comfort, but not the cheerful irreverence of Charles Hardcastle. He had seen and heard too much, and tonight it would not do. He went on along Church Lane, making briskly for the Bell. Inside there were lights and voices, and once more he hesitated. Then he went to the car and got in. It smelled of Cynthia, and a stab of reminiscent tenderness caught at his heartstrings. He started the engine, backed, turned, crept out into the street and set course for Frantham.

The road spun out smoothly in front of him in the headlights, and sanity began to seep back. Even so, he quailed at the crowded cheerfulness of the Antelope bar and went to look for somewhere quieter. He turned off the High Street, went between the windows of empty, unpretentious shops and turned again into a lane running parallel with the High Street. There were small terrace houses on one side and on the other the yard gates and goods entrances of the bigger shops. Another small street turned off between the houses, and he saw, almost over him, a lit sign which said The Rose. There was no picture and only masked lights. Just the floodlit sign and a shut door beneath.

He opened the door and went in. He was still undecided and went quietly. A glassed door on his right gave on to an amber-lit saloon bar. He put his hand to the handle and stopped. Mr. Garstin leaned on the bar, staring into an almost empty glass. The shoulders and back were immobile in a sagging line. This was the man John had left on the bridge at night, unable to find the resolution to go home and to bed. Next to him, a woman, much shorter than Garstin, stood with her back to the door, talking vehemently into the empty space behind the bar. There was no one else in the room. He could hear most of what she said but nothing of Garstin's replies, if, indeed, he made any.

The woman, leaning forward on the bar, put an elegantly shod foot behind her and pivoted it on its toe as she talked. She had nice legs, but he could not see her face at all. There was a glimpse of dark hair beyond the turned-up coat collar but nothing else. "I don't think I'm being unreasonable," she said. "I can't help it if I am. You've got to make up your mind. We can't go on as we are. I can't, anyhow."

Mr. Garstin drank what was left in his glass, but John did not think he tasted it. If he said anything, it was not audible. He put the empty glass down, and the girl spun suddenly to face him fully. John looked at the sleek, piled-up hair and the pale incisive profile for several seconds before he placed it. What was it Cynthia had said? Sheila, that was it. Sheila Drew, and she worked in the Upsindon estate office. Under, presumably, Mr. Garstin, or had he relinquished charge when he became prince consort? John had not thought to ask, and wished now he had. Neat but ruthless, Cynthia had said, taking over what he himself had said about the girl's driving. Neat she certainly was. Not quite a beauty, but with considerable style. The ruthlessness he could not answer for, but there was no mistaking the resolution. He could feel it, through the glass of the door, concentrated like a sun-lamp on the irresolute dejection of the man she was talking to.

He had missed something while she moved, but now she spoke up again. She said, "I've no scruples whatever. I can't afford them, not in this. I'd do anything. Dick, can't you see? You must see, surely?"

She put a hand out suddenly and laid it on Garstin's sleeve. He covered it with his own, and turned and smiled at her. It softened the drawn face into a surprising tenderness, and John

68

was conscious of a sudden wave of compassion, such as he had felt earlier for Derek. Mr. Garstin could have been, as George Curtis had said, a nice man. John, wavering behind his glass screen, could see the niceness there, but knew, even as he saw it, that no niceness would meet the present occasion. The next moment he moved, as quickly as he knew how.

Sheila Drew gathered herself together, picked up her bag from the top of the bar and turned and made for the door. John had just time to recognize, even as she was making it, that slight but deliberate movement of readjustment which the clothes-conscious woman makes before she gets under way. There was no time to go out on to the pavement, but at least he got himself away from the glass door and was making a decent show of coming in from outside when she opened the glass door and came out. Mercifully, she came alone, and did not know him. They met face to face between the doors. The face was broad and square-jawed, and the mouth, wickedly reddened in the pale face, too long for beauty but full of interest. For a long moment a pair of wide gray eyes under dark brows looked at him steadily. Then he gave the quick, impersonal smile politeness required and stood aside to let her pass. He heard the outer door shut behind him as she went out, hesitated a moment and then, keyed up to meet an unlucky chance, pushed open the glass door and went into the bar. There was no alternative. If there was one thing he was sure of, it was that Sheila Drew would remember she had seen him, and where.

He nodded casually to Garstin and then went into a fairly elaborate act of recognition. He said, "It's Mr. Garstin, isn't it?" The glass door had rung a bell somewhere as Sheila went out and again as he came in, and the lady of the house appeared behind the bar. He ordered himself a whiskey and turned to Garstin.

Seen at close range, he looked tired and very wary. He was

older than John had at first thought, almost certainly nearer forty than thirty. He said, "Yes, of course. We met for a moment at Upsindon." He was better, thought John, dealing with an immediate situation. Much of the indecisiveness had gone, and he was playing, from the start, a chosen gambit. He said, "You're staying in Coyle, aren't you?"

"That's right. I got held up going through, and have been there ever since. Mr. Hardcastle befriended me."

Garstin nodded. "Then you're being well looked after. And George Curtis will do his best for you." He paused, looked at his empty glass and decided against it. "How did you find the Rose?" he said. "It's a haunt of mine. I come here when I want to be quiet."

The eyes were a shade too small. They drilled into him, looking for a glimmer of hesitation. He had almost, John thought, said "want to be alone." He had implied it. John shrugged. "Pure chance. Same thing, really. I thought the Antelope looked a bit noisy, so I took the first turning I came to, and here I am."

The landlady brought John's whiskey, looked at Garstin, failed to catch his eye and withdrew. Haunt or no haunt, thought John, she did not know who Garstin was. Garstin said, "I'm not an awfully social type, in fact. I was afraid you must have thought—"

John waved it aside. "Not a bit. Your wife had suggested I might like to have a look round."

"Yes. It's her house, you see. I wonder whether—I really ought to be going, if you won't think it unfriendly."

John said, "Of course not," and Garstin nodded and went. The whiskey was oily and sharpish. It was not calculated to dispel the almost tangible unhappiness left hanging in the air. After a first sip he frowned and poured it straight down. He was tired and did not know what he was going to do with his evening.

70

CHAPTER 8

COYLE HAD LOST the sun again, but went about its business feverishly in the damp gloom. Excited voices talked behind shut doors or around the next corner of the street. But the doors stayed shut, or the speakers dispersed and hurried off on their own purposes as he came in sight, and John never heard what was being said. He could not mistake the gaiety, but could not share it. It was like being an adult at a very young party. He was missing something, but would not have it at the price.

He was beginning to see why, as Charles Hardcastle said, St. Udan's, Coyle, worked. It made, as far as he could see, few demands except active and cheerful participation; and once the thing was established, its power of conscious exclusion was very great. Only the real independents or the hard-case misfits stood out against it, and these it cheerfully ignored. Whatever Old Liberty believed in, he had the people whooping at his back. John, who knew that a world outside Coyle existed, and that Upsindon was part of it, discounted, but could not disperse, a growing apprehension.

The black car slid to a halt just ahead of him as he walked up toward the bridge, and Mrs. Garstin leaned across and threw the near-side door open. She did not turn her head until he came alongside her. When he did, she looked at him gravely and steadily. He felt that she was seeing him for the first time, whereas he had known her as far back as his memory went. She

71

said, "I want to talk to you. Can you come?"

He nodded and got in, and she drove on for a bit in silence. Presently she pulled in to the side of the road and stopped. There was a door he had not noticed set in an arch of the wall. She opened her bag in the pocket of the car and took out a key. Then she got out and went across the grass to the door. He followed her and stood while she opened the door. There was nothing on it but a latch lock. She threw the door open and stood aside. "Go on," she said.

He found himself in a belt of half-grown hardwoods, perhaps twenty yards deep. He could see a fence on the far side and open pasture beyond. She shut the door on the latch and came after him. She said, "I want to see what Richard has been doing with these trees." He had, immediately, the answer to the question he had asked himself in the Rose at Frantham. Richard was Mr. Garstin, and Mr. Garstin was still in charge of the estate office. He had acquired, presumably, some additional duties, but not, unless he mistook her tone, any noticeable change in status. She turned right and walked between the lines of trees. He walked beside her, and found that, for all the unhurried serenity of her movement, she set a good pace. They walked for a minute in silence. Then she nodded and stopped. He did not for a moment doubt that she had, as she said, come to see the trees. She said, "How old are you, Mr. Smith?"

"Twenty-six."

She nodded. "Derek is nineteen. You met him, didn't you?"

"For a moment, yes."

"After Father—after the vicar had gone?"

"That's right."

"What did you talk about?"

He hesitated, and she turned suddenly and took hold of him. She said, "Please. Please. I must know." Her eyes were hazel between dark lashes. Her skin had a touch of gold in it, and her dark hair had reddish lights. He did not think he liked her very much, but he knew that his hands were trembling as they held her, and that his voice, when he found it, would be husky with immediate need. He bent to kiss her, but she moved her head away from him. "Tell me," she said.

He said, "We—" He found his throat was dry and started again. "He said—he said he thought the vicar had come on business."

"What business?"

"He didn't say. He said he knew what the business was, but he didn't say what."

She loosened her hold on him and drew a little away. He let her go perforce, but her eyes held his. She said, "Was that all?" She pulled him to her again when he did not answer. "Was that all?" she said. "Was that all Derek said?"

He smiled down at her, momentarily secure in a masculine solidarity with Derek and with all subject males everywhere. "That's all," he said. He bent and kissed her, losing himself in the kiss. Everything about her was sensuously perfect. But when he opened his eyes, he had a sudden, uncomfortable feeling that hers had been open and watching him. She said, "It's not fair." She said it with the serious indignation of a child, so that he felt suddenly mean and wanted to comfort her.

He smiled at her and took refuge in a question. "What isn't fair?" he said. Exactly, he thought, as if she had been a child, and he was humoring her. But she would not look at him.

"They've no right," she said. It came straight from the heart, and he was immediately aware of a time when Mary Whatever-she-was had not been sitting on top of a liege world, but had cried out, as ordinary people cry out, against the injustice of a system that would not give her everything she wanted. She said again, almost to herself, "They've no right. They've got everything they want." She looked at him open-eyed, including him

73

in her indignation. Then she pulled herself out of his arms and started to walk back toward the door in the wall.

He went after her, stunned by an appalling sense of loss. He said lamely, "If there's anything I can do—" but she did not stop or turn around. As they came to the door he realized that from this side no key was needed, and went ahead and held it open for her. She looked at him, as she went through, with the same grave, considering look she had first turned on him in the car. All her indignation was gone. She said, "Only tell me the truth, Mr. Smith, that's all."

He found no reply to this. He shut the door after him and followed her to the car, but did not get in beside her. She sat for a moment, staring straight ahead while he stood and watched her. The only thing he consciously wanted was to take hold of her again, but in the back of his mind he was unwilling to pay the price, as he had, on the dark top of the tower, been unwilling to pay the price demanded for another sort of peace.

She suddenly gave a little laugh. "Oh dear," she said. "Do you mind walking home?"

"No, no. I was out for a walk anyhow."

"All right. Come and see me again, will you? You haven't met Richard—my husband—have you?"

"Just. But very casually." He wondered despairingly what he would do if she asked where, but she did not.

She merely nodded. "They're very different," she said, "he and Derek." Then she gave him a quick half-smile and was gone. He stood looking after the low black car until it disappeared around the bend. Then he turned and started walking back to Coyle.

When he had still some way to go, he thought he heard a single bell ringing from the church; but the village was completely quiet when he came back to it. There was no one about in the streets. The sky drooped like a tarpaulin, heavy with its own damp, across the top of the valley, so that he saw the tower as a central prop, carrying this vast additional burden on the flawed stonework of its base. The singing started suddenly when he was halfway up the steps, a tremendous burst of children's voices thrown up in delighted abandon at the overarching darkness. He went to the parapet and looked down. They were processing around the foot of the tower, trooping at any rate in an embryonic procession, children of all ages and shapes. Someone must be marshaling them, but from where he was he could see no larger figure. It was a shrill, jaunty tune with a piercing refrain, so piercing that he imagined it would vibrate in the cracks of the masonry and bring the whole lot down as the trumpets brought down Jericho. Only that was not what it was for. The children went around the three free-standing sides of the tower, countermarching like a regimental band where it joined the western arches of the nave. Whatever they sang, he could not hear a word.

A cold wave of apprehension gripped him, so that he wanted to lean over and shout to them to stop singing and stand clear before the stones came down on them. "He mustn't do it," he found himself saying, "he mustn't do it." But he could not have made himself heard, and it was all nonsense anyway. Only the choir trebles singing in the churchyard, in rehearsal for a more formal occasion to come. The singing stopped suddenly, dissolving into a babel of chatter as the children broke up and went off to their dinners. He walked on gloomily up the steps and found Cynthia leaning on the white gate at the top. She said, "That didn't take long. Saved by the bell?"

He said, "What in the world were those children up to?"

"Singing. Practicing for the festival."

"But singing what? Either something very primitive or something brand new. I couldn't make out."

"I don't know where Old Liberty gets them from. I sometimes

think he makes them up. Could he have?"

"I don't see why not, given a natural ear and no knowledge of music—and a sufficiently unsophisticated mind. No wonder the children like it. But what were they doing?"

She looked at him, still standing on the far side of the gate. She said, "I reckon singing the tower up, don't you?"

"I suppose so. I thought at one moment they were singing it down."

"Those innocents?"

He shook his head. "The tower of Siloam," he said.

She opened the gate. "You won't—you won't talk about this to Daddy, will you?"

"I won't, I promise."

"Right. Now come in and tell me about Round Two."

They walked across the terrace and sat on the coping of the wall. He sighed. "I'd much rather not," he said.

"I know. But I'd much rather you did. Exorcism, if nothing else. And you promised, didn't you?"

"I kissed her," he said.

"By invitation, by accident or willy-nilly?"

"I don't know. I honestly don't know. But willy-nilly, in any case."

"And it's—it's shaken you a bit, hasn't it?"

"Yes. Yes, but—I'm not sure, but I don't think I like her. I thought at first I might be going to like her in spite of herself. Now I'm inclined to think the boot's on the other foot." He beat his clenched hand rhythmically on his knee where it rested on the edge of the wall. "I don't really expect you to understand," he said.

"Don't you? I don't see why not. I've known Lady Potiphar quite a while."

He gave her a rather despairing smile. "I think that is less than just," he said.

"Probably. Jokes often are."

He got up and stood over her as she sat staring down at Coyle. He said, "But injustice isn't your line. I think you have an interest to declare." He smiled again, but she did not see it. "Exorcism, if nothing else," he said.

She turned him a face of such woe that his heart seemed to miss a beat. "I love Dick Garstin," she said. "You know that, don't you?"

They looked at each other long and steadily. Then he shook his head. "Not really," he said. "Not now."

She considered this carefully and without protest, but did not answer it. "All the same," she said, "the interest is there. I think you are right not to like her."

"But I don't very much dislike her. I mean—she's not straight bitch, you know."

"I know that, of course. Bitches are two a penny. Mary Garstin's a lot more expensive than that." She looked at him in that curiously direct and analytical way she had borrowed from her father but used so much more damagingly. She said, "Perhaps I don't understand very well, in fact. If you don't like her, but don't think she's a bitch, why do you have to kiss her?"

"It's an impersonal business. You feel the warmth of the fire and you spread out your hands to it instinctively. When the fire isn't there, you don't miss it. You don't even remember it very clearly. There must be a Mrs. Garstin inside that splendid phenomenon. At least, I suppose there must. But either it's very carefully hidden or it's very—I don't know, very small, perhaps very young and undeveloped. I may be wrong about this, but I don't think you hate her, do you? Not as you'd hate an ordinary bitch?"

She did not answer for some time, and when she spoke, she spoke with her eyes fixed steadily on the top of the tower. She said, "I don't hate her, but I dislike very much what she does. I think it would be much better if she wasn't there. I don't hate an influenza germ. Perhaps because it's very small or very well hidden. But I kill it if I can."

The door of the house opened, and Mr. Hardcastle came out on to the terrace. He gave the impression of making an entrance, and John had the uncomfortable feeling that he had been hovering tactfully inside, awaiting the appropriate moment. But he was kindness itself. He said, "Isn't it time we had a drink and some food? It's a miserable day, and we lack the spiritual glow that sustains our neighbors. Speaking for myself, anyhow. Come on in, both of you, for goodness' sake."

Over the meal he said, "I saw Old Liberty today. I should say he was in a highly frenetic state. His head was so far in front of the rest of him that he hardly seemed to have his feet on the ground. Like Alice in the grip of the Red Queen, you know?"

"The festival?" said John.

"I suppose so. But the festival is a symptom, not the disease itself. It is the disease which seems to be working up to some sort of crisis. I may be imagining it. He didn't say much. He seldom does to me."

"Is that hostility? Or fear? Or can he simply not be bothered?"

"Not really hostility, I don't think. Mistrust, perhaps. He senses a mental opposition he doesn't understand, and that makes him wary. But he much prefers to pass it by. So we exchange nothings for the sake of saying something. It's disconcerting until you get used to it."

"That's what Derek Potter said, more or less. That Father Freeman never seemed quite to recognize his existence. Disconcerting was his word for it, too."

"Yes—well, another case, do you see? Derek is another person Old Liberty can't digest."

"One of the clever ones?" said John.

78

"Yes—yes, I can imagine that represents his attitude. I've never actually heard him say it. But I'm sure there is that sort of resentment there. I think the power he exercises over simpler souls makes him resent its failure with others."

John smiled. "The command of allegiance that becomes an addiction?" he said.

"Ah. There might be an interesting parallel there, yes."

"And on your theory an interesting contest, don't you think?"

"A struggle for power? Yes." But Mr. Hardcastle was not satisfied. "But it's a personal relation, isn't it?" he said. "They're not contesting their power over other people. They're contesting their power over each other. On my theory," he added with conscious magnanimity, "always on my theory."

Cynthia said, "If it's the vicar and Mrs. Garstin you're talking about, the odd thing is surely that they exercise any power over each other at all. I don't think they do, in fact. There's some sort of a bargain to be struck. But I'm not sure what the commodities involved are." She smiled suddenly at her father with huge and tolerant affection. "I'm sorry about your theory," she said. "I'm sure it was a nice one."

He waved her down with his familiar deprecating gesture and repeated the formula John had already heard. "Speculation," he said, "only speculation. But enjoyable."

Mr. Hardcastle vanished into the house and John and Cynthia came out on to the terrace. He said, "You're wrong, you know. I don't mind how much you dislike my saying it. You're barking up the wrong tree."

"I'm not barking up any tree. I shouldn't do anything so vulgar." But the joke got no further than the words, and she looked at John with apprehensive green eyes, wondering what he was going to say next.

He said, "How long have you known Richard Garstin?"

"Since he came here."

"And how old were you then?"

"I was—I was at school."

"But you're not at school now. And you're a remarkable person, do you remember?"

She nodded and managed a faint smile.

"Well," he said, "use your loaf, for God's sake."

"But—" She bit her lip, staring out over Coyle to the trees that hid Upsindon. "You don't know the kind of pressure he's under."

"Miss Drew?"

She whipped around to face him. "Sheila? Why her rather than—than the other one?"

"Because that's where the pressure comes from. You know that, don't you? I do if you don't. But in fact I think you do, only perhaps you won't face it. That's what I mean when I say use your loaf."

He turned and walked toward the gate, but she went with him. She said, "And you yours, if it comes to that. The next time you feel the warmth of the fire, better keep your hands in your pockets, don't you think?"

He stood and faced her by the gate. "No more round-by-round commentary?" he said.

She looked at him somberly. "No more rounds," she said.

He nodded and went down the steps, full of an unexpected assurance.

CHAPTER 9

GEORGE CURTIS SAID, "You met Mr. Garstin, did you?"

It was so plainly a statement rather than a question that John saw no need to hedge. He said, "Yes, in Frantham the other evening. Place called the Rose. It was pure chance actually. I walked in and there he was."

The intelligent, rather troubled eyes watched him for a moment to see if he was going on. When he did not, the little man nodded. He said, "He's a nice man, Mr. Garstin" exactly as he had said it before. Only then, John remembered, there had been a "but."

It was John's turn to wait, and he waited while George Curtis made up his mind. Finally he took the plunge. "We never expected him to marry Lady Potter," he said.

"Or Lady Potter to marry him?" said John, and got a flash of grateful recognition from the watchful eyes.

"That's it. But I suppose—I mean, he'd been with them a year or two, seeing a lot of both of them. It was natural enough, I suppose. Only we thought he'd be marrying Miss Drew."

Once more John waited, his face elaborately blank. And once more George Curtis made his decision and went on. "Miss Drew was working with Mr. Garstin at Upsindon, in the office. They weren't engaged, but we reckoned there was an understanding, even after Sir Gerald was dead. But then her ladyship decided different."

81

It was a masterpiece of neutrality, perfectly calculated at dead center between the ecstatic "your ladyship" of Mrs. Curtis and the ironic "her ladyship" which John felt sure George Curtis would apply to a spoiled little girl. This simply stated the fact with no overtones. It had been the boss's decision. Lady Potiphar's, he thought, and then reminded himself that he had told Cynthia that this was unjust. He waited for the next step, but none came. Then George Curtis, as he had before, sighed and, sighing, gave him his cue. He took it boldly. "And it hasn't turned out well?" he said.

George Curtis spoke up with sudden, unmistakable bitterness, and then immediately muted it. "She's got what she wants," he said. "I suppose," he added. "And there's Mr. Garstin still working in the office, and Miss Drew still working with him. I suppose Mrs. Garstin knows how she stands." He looked at John with a sharp quizzical eye. "Well," he said, "you've met her."

So that's it, thought John. Somebody else wants a round-by-round commentary, or something very like it. It did not occu· to him for a moment to hedge, only he did not know what it would be true to say. Finally he said, "I don't think I know what she does want." And I wonder, he thought, why I can talk straighter to George Curtis than I can to Charles Hardcastle. "But for what it's worth," he said, "I don't think I should feel at all sure she's got it."

George Curtis said, "Ah," and they both, without batting an eye, heard Mrs. Curtis come into the kitchen behind the bar. John drank his beer and wondered, when he had rolled down the hill toward Coyle in his gravity-propelled car, what role he had been cast for. The *deus ex machina*, he thought; but that wasn't quite fair. Jokes, as Cynthia had said, very often weren't. But a catalyst of some sort, surely. Not someone to set things right by his own decision, but something to unsettle them by upsetting a delicately established balance. That was what more than one person expected of him. He was not at all sure he liked the part.

There was a sudden babel of young voices, mixed with bursts of rather hysterical laughter. It brought him up all standing. The landlord had gone through into the kitchen, and John went to the window, flattening his nose against the glass as he had to see Mrs. Garstin go off in her big car. The street seemed to be be full of girls. They were all carrying sticks. As they came nearer, they resolved themselves into an untidy procession, moving three or four abreast along the street. They certainly did not march, but they kept moving with a sort of casual purposiveness, like cows coming in unherded to the milking shed. They moved under a running fire of male ribaldry from both sides of the street. Some of the shrewder hits registered on particular parts of the column in shrieks of protest, but for the most part they merely looked down their noses and smiled. They were enjoying themselves no end. They held their sticks shoulder high, pointing resolutely upward as they went along.

John, running an expert and appreciative eye over them as they drifted past, found the landlord at his elbow. Disguise being neither possible nor necessary, they exchanged ribald glances. "Girls' Friendly," said George Curtis. John, none the wiser, nodded knowingly, and returned to the study of form, until the column was brought up by two ripe beauties who seemed, unless he was much mistaken, to be advanced candidates for admission to the Mothers' Union.

He turned back to the bar. "But what—?" he said. "Why the sticks?"

"Torches, they'll be, on the night. All the lot carrying torches. It'll be quite a sight, I must say."

"Good lord alive. A fire festival."

"Well, it is that, really. Of course, we always had a bonfire up on the tump, but the torchlight procession is Mr. Freeman's idea. Mind you, they'll enjoy it all right, so long as no one gets burnt."

John put his tankard down on the bar and leaned his head on his hands. "Always?" he said. "When you say always, how long has this been going on?"

"Well, like I say. We've always had a bonfire on the tenth. It's our Bonfire Night, if you see. Then the vicar gets the idea of making it a church affair, and now we're having the procession and all the rest of it. But as I say, they'll enjoy it. There won't be any less girls getting into trouble, I dare say, even if they do start from the church."

John whistled. "That old trick? Medieval, Mr. Hardcastle said. Medieval my foot. It's the early fathers. What you can't eradicate, adopt. If they must have Yule, at least call it Christmas. But a girl can't get into trouble with a burning torch in her hand, surely? At least—" He lost himself in speculation.

George Curtis said gloomily, "The torches go out, you see. And then there's dancing and all the rest." He brought his full powers of implication to bear.

John nodded solemnly. "The torches go out," he said. "They must sometime, of course."

The landlord smiled with a sudden ribald cheerfulness and repeated his assurance. "But they'll enjoy themselves," he said.

John, staring into the gloom behind the bar, said, "So long as no one gets burnt." He said it almost under his breath, weighed down again with his intolerable apprehension. The friendly girls had gone, and the village was very quiet.

"A gin for you?" said George Curtis, but John shook his head. "No thank you," he said, "no gin today." He shook himself like a dog coming out of cold water, and went out into the street. He hesitated there and then went back into the bar. "Mr. Curtis!" he called. "Mr. Curtis, are you there?" In the kitchen he heard Mrs. Curtis say, "It isn't right. It isn't right." Then she broke off and Mr. Curtis put his head through the intervening door. John said, "Where is the tump?"

"The tump? Right when you get outside, as if you were going to Frantham. Then there's a turning off left. Round the end of the church, it goes. You'll see it. Or you can ask. St. Anne's Hill," he said, and threw his head back impatiently. "St. Anne's Hill, they call it now. But you'll see it, I reckon."

John thanked him and went out. It was as cloudy as ever and very still. He turned toward Frantham, passed the end of Church Lane and went on until he came to the end of the houses. He had come this way only once, and then his mind had been occupied by the side view of his driver and the breathless insouciance of her driving. Now he saw what he had not noticed before. The main road ran close to the right-hand side of the valley, winding around the contour under the overhanging trees. But to the left the valley opened out beyond the village, and a lane, as George Curtis had said, led off almost under the eastern end of the churchyard. It followed the contour as the main road did, and before long an east-facing slope of the Gale closed down and merged itself with the left-hand hedgerow. In front a shallow basin of meadowland opened up, rising at its center to a conical green hill. A low saddle, which the lane must cross, connected it with the main hillside, but the cone itself and the saddle for most of its length were clear of trees. It was beautifully regular from where he saw it, but certainly natural. Only at its apex a green nipple stood up against the dark background of trees; and here certainly the hand of man was apparent, though whose hand and of what period he could not tell. Even as he looked, figures moved on it and something broke the rounded outline of the turf. Whoever had raised the mound, man was at work on it again.

He went along the roughly metaled lane, and presently a field gate opened in the hedge on his right. The gate stood

85

wide, and the broad marks of tractor tires led off in a curve across the grass, making around the eastern flank of the hill. He could hear voices now from the top of the slope above him. They were men's voices, but from here the men themselves were out of sight. The tracks spiraled cannily up the green slope, until quite suddenly he came out over the shoulder of the hill and saw what was going on. They were building the fire.

It was a scene of tremendous activity, cheerful but perfectly serious. They were a long way, here, from the self-conscious sauntering of the friendly girls and the shrill ecstasy of the singing children. Men at work, thought John. He was struck momentarily with something like dismay at the comprehensive effectiveness of the vicar's dispositions. Barring the disregarded outsiders, everybody was involved, and involved at his own level of intelligence and enjoyment. Boys, he knew, built village bonfires for weeks before Guy Fawkes Day, bringing in combustibles of every sort from every direction and heaping them up in an ill-digested pile that generally burned in the end if it did not get too wet first. John had done it himself and, later, seen it done in half a dozen places. But this was quite different. A very old man, wielding a long gray staff like a latter-day leech-gatherer, was in quiet but effective command. He probably, thought John, rang the tenor bell on Sundays, using his dried-out weight with the same unhurried efficiency on the surging sally. All around him younger men fetched and carried, placed, shifted and replaced the cut wood nearer to his old heart's desire and the precise picture his accumulated experience gave him of the perfect fire. The old man turned and looked at him as he came hesitantly up the slope, and for a moment John half expected him to point his staff at him and say *"Procul este, profani."* Instead he merely looked at him, carefully and at length, and then turned and went on with his operation.

A sense of familiarity gripped him, as if somewhere, at some time, if only in his mind, he had seen the whole thing before. Then a phrase floated into his conscious mind, and he knew what he was after. The pyre of Hector. It was not a bonfire these people were building. It was a pyre. Something of value was ripe for translation into flame. The job was a serious one and had to be done properly. He stood there, just over the shoulder of the hill, unrebuked but unregarded, and watched the work go on under the gray sky. Then he turned and, still full of uneasiness, went slowly down the hill.

He did not know the car at the time, but remembered it afterward. It came slowly along the lane—it occurred to him that he did not know where the lane went to—moving toward Coyle. When he was still some way from the gate, the car stopped just clear of it and he saw the far door open. The hedge intervened, and he could not see if anyone got out. He walked on steadily toward the gate and then, as he turned out into the lane, came face to face with Sheila Drew.

He never for a moment doubted that she knew him—not merely knew him as a remembered face, but knew who he was. Garstin had certainly told her about their meeting in the Rose. For his own part, John allowed himself to look at her with interest. She was indeed very interesting to look at. If a suggestion of recognition got into the look, this did not matter. She would, he thought, be used to being remembered. What he did not expect was the extent to which the meeting disconcerted her. Her vivid powerful face was well exercised in self-control, but her legs betrayed her, wavering and almost coming to a halt at the sight of him coming to meet her. But she came on, head up and eyes straight ahead, and at the appropriate distance suddenly smiled at him. It was, as he remembered it afterward, a brilliant smile, lighting up unexpectedly a naturally serious face. She was a girl, he thought, one would do a great deal for, if only to win the recognition of that sudden smile.

87

She said, "How's it going?"

He recognized the calculated ambivalence of the question, and rejected, in the light of those wide gray eyes, any attempt at subtlety. "Busy as bees," he said. "Who's the ancient in charge?"

"That will be Elias Meadows. But don't be misled by the name. He is a retired debt-collector, and as hard as nails. Only he does understand fires. If you gave him a bunch of iron bedsteads, he'd stack them so that you only had to put a match to them. And of course he'll dope it nearer the time. It will burn all right. You'll see. How far have they got?"

"I'm not in the Elias Meadows class. But I'd say there's a good deal more material to come. The tractor's not there. I imagine there's another load on the way. But I don't know how much they bring up at a time. It's a pretty tricky slope."

"Nothing to what it can be, I assure you. It's chalk under the grass. Get it thoroughly wet and scuff it up a bit, and you could practically ski on it. But it's pretty dry at the moment. Why are you so interested?"

He found the direct question disconcerting. She was no longer smiling, but watching him with an almost painful intensity. He said, "I think I'm interested in what the vicar's making of it all."

"Have you spoken to the vicar about it?"

"About the festival? No."

"Then—"

"George Curtis, mainly. And I've seen the preparations, of course."

"Mrs. Garstin?"

"Do you mean have I spoken to Mrs. Garstin about the festival?"

"Yes. Yes." The merest suggestion of prevarication seemed to gall her, so that she almost stamped her foot with impatience.

He smiled at her indignation. "Have you?" he said.

88

She seemed as unconscious of his provocation as she was of her own impatience. She said perfectly seriously, "I never speak to Mrs. Garstin about anything."

"No?" he said. "No, since you ask, I haven't." He nodded and went out into the lane, leaving her just inside the gate. He walked steadily toward the village and did not look back. He felt fairly certain that she was watching him, but equally certain that if he did turn, however suddenly, he would find her walking up the hill. He reached the village, went along the street and turned into Church Lane, but at no point did the small saloon catch him up.

"St. Anne's Hill?" said Charles Hardcastle later. "George Curtis is quite right to sniff at it, of course. Tan Hill, it should be. The map's littered with Tan Hills, and half of them have been christianized into St. Anne's. Fire Hill it means, or so I'm told. But whether they're beacons, or village junketing centers, or something more numinous is up to you. Like St. Udan—it depends whether you're of the pagan school. The tump, of course, is the tumulus on top. I don't think that's been looked at, but it needn't be anything very old. Anyway, it's the traditional bonfire site. George Curtis is right there. You've got to hand it to Old Liberty, though, haven't you? He makes it work."

"I think—to be honest, I find it all a bit disturbing. A man who can take over a local uphelya and turn it into a saint's-day celebration is capable of anything. And I can't see, yet, what he does with it."

Charles Hardcastle hesitated. "I can't tell you," he said. "I simply don't think I'm capable of judging. I see it only from the outside, do you see? Clearly and in detail, from a ringside seat. But always from the outside. Cynthia can tell you more than I can. I wondered whether you'd understood that."

"Yes," said John, "yes, I think so. But I haven't really put it to her."

They looked at each other gravely for a moment. Then Mr.

89

Hardcastle said, "Don't let yourself be misled by the hard casing, will you? Or by the fact that she talks about me as if I was an educationally subnormal senile delinquent. There is a great deal of old-fashioned good in the girl."

John said, "There is a great deal of old-fashioned silliness."

"Ah. Good. I am glad. I think we probably both mean the same thing, in fact. Only at my age and in my relation I can put a milder gloss on it. But about Old Liberty. All I can see, from my viewpoint, is that people are on the whole the happier for it. But I doubt whether that answers your question."

John frowned. "No," he said. "No, that's the trouble. I don't think it does."

CHAPTER 10

BEING YOUNG and human, John noticed the girl's legs before he
took in anything else. Her back was toward him, and she leaned
over, almost head down under the bonnet of the car. The skirt,
which would have been perfectly adequate in other circum-
stances, was not fully equal to the demands made upon it, and
there was a great deal of leg to look at. And very nice too, he
thought. Then two heads bobbed up together from over the
engine, and he saw that the one on his side was Cynthia Hardcastle's. A wave of emotion engulfed him, oddly compounded
of guilt and a pleasurable glow. It had not, somehow, occurred
to him what splendid legs she had and how much there was of
them. What had been a warm but romantic attraction took on
suddenly a sharper physical edge, and he was in two minds what
to make of it. Then he saw simultaneously that Cynthia was
looking at him a little severely and that the head on the other
side of the car belonged to Derek Potter.

It was Derek's car. He had no doubt at all about that. It was a
young man's car, but a good deal soberer than his own, a mod-
est but purposeful saloon, far from young but not old enough to
be rakish. It fitted the picture he had begun to form of Derek,
and at the same time improved it. But it was Cynthia he had, at
the moment, to deal with. The severity was still there, but as he
came to her, she began unexpectedly to blush. She blushed briefly
but thoroughly, looking at him out of her glowing face with star-

like, indignant eyes, so that his whole heart turned over. Beyond her Derek's face was blank, watchful but not noticeably hostile.

John said, "What is it this time? Another distributor lead?"

"No, no. She's going, but she's not going right. I think it's carburetor, but I'm not awfully good with carburetors." She turned to Derek. "George is a wizard with carburetors," she said. "Why not let him have a go?"

"I will if it doesn't right itself. Half the symptoms she develops disappear if I leave them long enough. At least, I think they do. Perhaps I just get used to them."

Cynthia said, "Do you ever ask Denton?"

"Denton? Christ, no. He doesn't know she exists. He's far too busy polishing the Daimler. In any case, I shouldn't think he knows. Why should he? Nothing ever goes wrong with the family cars."

"What does he do with his time, then? There's next to no routine servicing now, and your mother drives herself half the time."

Derek grinned savagely. "I know what he does with his time. Same as everybody else. It's the boss's time he couldn't account for. I don't know why my mother keeps him—or the Daimler. We never had a chauffeur in my father's time. And there's lots of other things she could spend the money on. Me, for one."

Cynthia said to John, "Derek is the poor little rich boy. Did you know?"

"I had rather suspected it, yes."

"That's right," said Derek. "Always tearing about in expensive sports cars and smashing them up on the family insurance." He kicked the saloon affectionately. It gave out a hollow clang, but did not budge. "Expensive sports cars," he said.

"Well, it would go much better if you'd have that carburetor sorted," said Cynthia. "I'll tell George, and the next time—"

"You leave it to me," said Derek. "I like to feel the imperfections of my environment."

"Oh all right, all right. Wallow in your misery, if that's what you want. But don't blame me if one of these days you have to walk home."

"Don't worry. I'll send a wire to Denton to come and fetch the young master from the roadside. But thank you for your diagnosis, anyway. I'm sure you're right, as usual. One of these days I'll buy a handbook and be able to do it all myself."

"Well, you know, you really ought to. You're a scientist, aren't you?"

Derek looked at her carefully. He came to the conclusion that she was serious, and spoke gently out of the vast reservoir of primordial male patience. "I am a chemist," he said. "I am concerned, ultimately, with the infinite permutations of the elements. Tuning carburetors isn't part of the course."

"Sorry." She smiled at him affectionately, giving him back patience for patience. "Anyway, I must be going. I hope the carburetor holds up." She divided a goodbye scrupulously between them and went off down the road, walking short and quick in her perfectly adequate skirt.

For a moment the two young men watched her go. Then Derek turned to John and said, "Sorry if I was a bit short with you the other day. I thought you were just another of my mother's call-ups, although I had my doubts later. But Cynthia gives you a good character, and she's generally right. Are you going my way?"

"I wasn't really going anywhere. But if you'll drop me at the gate, I'll walk home. It's just about the distance I need."

Derek nodded. "Get in, then," he said. He shut down the bonnet flap with a clang and got into the driving seat.

John said, "As a matter of fact, I wouldn't say you were wrong. The other day, I mean. I met your mother by chance at the gate, and she simply brought me along."

"At least," said Derek, "she's never flirted with me. I have that to be very considerably thankful for."

"I don't think she flirts with anybody. She isn't that sort of person at all."

"No, I know. That's what I mean. I've seen so many pretty mums—any school half-term would bring out half a dozen of them in their best hats—fluttering their eyelashes alternately at the boy and his dad, and making both of them throw chests and buzz around seeing that Mum was comfortable. Dad was nearly always, I noticed, of the same mental age group as the boy. I suppose that's why he fell for it. And of course I knew the sons too, pretty well, some of them."

"Me too," said John gloomily.

"Yes, well, you know what I'm talking about. To do her justice, my mother's never done that to me. On the contrary, the difficulty has generally been to remind her that I exist at all. But it's the better of the two extremes, of course. If one has to go to extremes." He thought for a bit, driving soberly in his sober car. Then he said, "Of course, with my father it was all right. He knew exactly where he was with her. He knew what he wanted from her and what he could expect."

John said, "Yes, well that's it, do you see? Your pretty little eyelash flutterer has a relation with men generally in which her son can perfectly well be included. Your mother hasn't. She isn't feminine at all—not in the way it's generally used. She is entirely female. I wonder what she'd have made of a daughter. You're the only one, I take it?" Derek nodded. "A pity in a way. A girl with your father's brains and your mother's female qualities would have been quite something. Only she might well have made worse trouble for you, I suppose."

"I don't think it could happen," said Derek. "My mother's whole make-up requires an almost total lack of intellect. Not of

94

intelligence—she's quite intelligent. But give her an intellect, and the whole picture would change completely."

"Yes. Yes, as a matter of fact, I think you're right."

"At any rate," said Derek, "it would remove the menace of Old Liberty. At least, I think so. I don't really know, because I really know very little about her as a person. I came to the conclusion long ago that there was only one effective channel of communication, and that was, naturally, not open to me. I felt this very clearly, even when my father was alive. I never actually discussed it with him, but he knew all right. I mean, he knew I understood."

"Yes," said John, "but, you know, even given that channel of communication, one's understanding of her remains very slight. I have a very vivid picture of her, but I can't reconcile it with her apparent relation with Father Freeman. And I did see them together, if you remember."

"Well, believe me, if I knew what hidden spring Old Liberty touches, I'd untouch it. But I don't. She lacks power over him, of course, which helps. But that's not it."

After a bit John said, "It's no business of mine, but we did refer to it—obliquely, anyhow. The menace is, I imagine, his trying to get money out of her for his tower?"

"I imagine so, of course. We all imagine so. That seems to be the only thing he minds about. And he can't get the money anywhere else, not in a hundred years."

"Can he get it from her? I mean—can she afford it?"

"The whole lump? Good God, of course she can't afford it. We can't, anyway. I mean, she may actually have it, in a reasonably liquid form. And she has the legal right to throw it in the sea if she wants to. But to throw herself in would be just as sensible. If not more so. And much more considerate."

John said, "It's a big place, isn't it? I don't know the extent of it, but it must be worth a lot."

"Oh, certainly. But the place isn't hers. I mean, not to muck about with. It's tied up good and tight. For me, ultimately. Not that I'm dead keen, to be honest. But it's the liquid capital that's the point. That's what we've got to live on, and what Dick Garstin's got to run the place on. There's not all that much of it, considering. And she chucks it around a bit, as it is. Not in my direction, unfortunately."

"I see. So—if she were to let the vicar have what he wants, it would be pretty serious?"

"It would be disastrous. Dick Garstin knows that as well as I do. But I don't think he can do much about it. In fact, I know he can't. No, we must hope for the best. I don't think she's committed. In fact, I know she isn't, from the way Old Liberty's buzzing round. She may simply not be such a fool. Or something may happen to stop it. But I don't know what." He shook his head, staring straight in front of him along the darkening road. "I don't like the look of things," he said, "and that's a fact. Now less than ever."

He pulled the car in toward the gates and stopped there. John said, "Why now, particularly?"

"Well—this saint's-day festival. If I'm right, he's deliberately getting everybody steamed up to bursting point. Including, so far as he can, my mother, only she doesn't burst easily. But, given enough mass emotion, anything can happen. You know that. If he can bring her pretty close to the mark, and then get her into the middle of the highly hysterical faithful—you haven't heard them sing, have you? Not the whole lot together? It's very frightening. At least, to me it is. But if he could do that, and then get her to make an announcement—do you see? Or some maneuver like that. There's no knowing what she might not commit herself to. And she wouldn't take it back, whatever she felt about it next day."

"Do you really think that's what he's up to?"

96

"Good God, I don't know. But I fancy she's expected to open the ball in some way or other. All right, that may be just the usual thing—the lady of the manor opening the village fete. But unless I'm very much mistaken, he's expecting her to do a lot more afterwards than buy a pot of home-made marmalade and have a go at the hoop-la. I don't know, of course. And anyway, there's nothing I can do about it. At least, I haven't thought of anything so far."

John nodded glumly and got out. He went around to Derek's side of the car. "Thank you for the ride," he said. "I'm very glad we met—I mean, met again, properly."

Derek said, "Thank Cynthia really." He looked up at John with a cold blue eye, very calculating and managerial, an obvious inheritance from the successful Sir Gerald. He said, "What about Cynthia, anyway?"

John, looking down at him from his seven years' seniority, was nevertheless conscious of being asked his intentions and of the emotional confusion such a question produces even in the most innocent. He said, "What about her?" but it did not sound convincing.

Derek jerked his head impatiently. "Well—she likes you. It's time she got fixed on someone instead of mooning round after Dick. There is a queue ahead of her there, anyway. Only she bruises a bit easy, you know. You want to be careful."

John said, "How old is she?"

"Twenty. Nearly twenty-one. Eighteen months older than I am."

John nodded. "And what do you want me to say?"

"Say? I don't want you to say anything. I'm only pointing out the position."

"I don't know," said John. "I ought to want to knock your block off, but I can't say I do. I note your warning and will try to bear it in mind. Will that do?"

Derek started his engine. "Don't be such a bloody fool," he said. "That girl's worth six of you any day." He gave John another flash of frosty blue. "Well," he said, trying to be fair, "three, anyway."

John grinned at him suddenly. "All right, all right," he said. "Let me work out my own equations."

Derek's indignant stare melted suddenly to a lop-sided smile. "All right," he said. He let in the clutch and was gone. John walked back toward Coyle. He walked slowly, with his head bent and his hands behind his back. He tried to think constructively, but thought mostly of Cynthia. Not, except intermittently, her enchanting legs, but her eyes, peridot green in a flushed face, staring indignantly at the sudden revelation of a new and harsher reality between them. He could not get it out of his mind. He wanted very badly to see her again, but did not know what he would say to her when he did. At intervals his mind threw up an altogether more disturbing picture of a small figure, her mystery lost and her authority taken away, towered over by a gangling glass-eyed man in the middle of a singing mob, under compulsive pressure to do something she might be sorry for when the singing had stopped and the people had all gone home. He did not know how much of this Derek Potter had imagined, but he did not like the way his own mind seized on it. He walked into Coyle just before opening time and found George Curtis alone in the bar.

He gave John his drink and said, "So you went up to the tump, then?"

"Not all the way, quite. Near enough to see what they were doing. They were making a job of it, I must say. A chap called Meadows in charge of operations."

"Old Elias? He's always done it."

"Is he a bell-ringer, by any chance?"

"What—up there?" George Curtis jerked his head comprehensively skyward. "Not him. The only bells Elias ever rung were doorbells. He rung plenty of those. Only mostly he wasn't welcome. No. Elias is doing the fire because he's always done it. Be the same if it was a barbecue or a rock-and-roll session. Mind you, he does it well."

John nodded. He remembered now what Sheila Drew had said. He buried regretfully his picture of Elias Meadows as an elder of the church and said, "They're doing it in good time, aren't they? It must be all set up by now. What happens if it rains?"

"Rain? Rain wouldn't hurt the fire, not the way Elias builds them. It'll burn all right, rain or no rain."

"Then what's to prevent somebody's going up there in the meantime and setting it off? It's always happening with Guy Fawkes bonfires. The kids spend weeks building the fire ready for the fifth, and then some sod comes along a couple of nights early and puts a match to it."

George Curtis looked at him incredulously. "What, someone go up and light it before the tenth?"

"Well, they could, couldn't they—if it's all that well laid."

A small smile played round George Curtis's mouth as he shook his head, but his eyes were still scandalized. "You won't find anyone going up on the tump at night," he said, "not any of us. Not by themselves. Not if you paid them. Specially with the tenth coming on and the fire laid." He mopped the bar, still looking at John, and threw the cloth into the sink with a soft thud. "The fire will be there and ready on the tenth," he said. "And it will burn. You'll see."

He turned and went through into the kitchen, shutting the door behind him.

CHAPTER 11

THE NINTH broke clear and still. The sun brought up the vapors from the sodden greenery, and Coyle, swimming in a pool of golden mist, worked itself up audibly and deliberately for the excitements of the tenth. There seemed to be people singing everywhere, singly or in chorus. They sang tunes which John, hearing them fragmentarily and from a distance, found bewilderingly familiar. But he could never remember them afterward, and the words he could not catch at all. Outlandish figures hovered in doorways as he passed, but he could not decide whether they wore fancy dress or were merely the local youth got up to kill in the strange Italianate fashions of the day. Somebody somewhere, perhaps Elias Meadows, had been experimenting with torches, and a smell of burning pitch mixed itself with the vaporous sunlight. It caught at the back of his throat, increasing his uneasiness.

No one sang in the churchyard. The tower stood up in the yellow silence, motionless except to the mind's eye that saw the hair-cracks pullulate as the stresses crept between the stones. In 1880, according to the list of incumbents that hung inside the south door, the vicar had been the Reverend James Arbuthnot, M.A. Oxon. He had started all this, and John wondered what he would have made of it. Someone else—the Rowlands of Upsindon, as likely as not—had put up the money, but it had been the Reverend James's decision. The vicar is, and has always been, very much captain of his ship. A successor calling himself Father anything would have been shock enough. The man himself would have strained his faith to the breaking point. But the skilled, time-served masons who had done this slow murder and the respectful parishioners who had watched it from below— would they have sung for the Reverend James Arbuthnot as Coyle now sang for Father Freeman? Not, certainly, with their hearts in their mouths and to tunes that sounded like fifteenth-century revivalist hymns. Something was working to hold the top on St. Udan's tower which the man who had put it there had certainly never reckoned with. What it was John still did not know. Only, as Charles Hardcastle had said, it worked, and with a kind of ecstatic violence which galled his civilized instincts, but which he could not deride. He shook his head and went on slowly. He went on up the steps, wondering whether he would find, in this gold-washed morning, the new Cynthia, disturbed and disturbing, he had parted with on the dark afternoon before. But when he came to the top, he knew he need not have worried. Cynthia was not there.

Charles Hardcastle was on the terrace, snuffing the air and peering into the haze below. He said, "The devil smells of gunpowder, or so they say. Am I imagining it, or is there something in the air?"

"It will be the torches, won't it?"

"Oh that, of course. I had forgotten. A pair of sacks steeped in tar oil and wired tight on a three-foot length of two-by-two. Or so I am told. That is the man-size job, anyway. I imagine the women and children carry something less formidable. And the St. John's Ambulance section will be in attendance. We are point-devise in our accouterments and have all the unshakable logic of lunacy. I wonder if the weather will hold."

"Unless, as you said, the opposition wishes foul weather on them."

101

Charles Hardcastle looked at him somberly. "I wish them a downpour," he said. "But I doubt if I shall get it."

"But why?" said John. "You once said—I think the first time we met, in fact—you said you liked to see the fun. From the sidelines, admittedly, but you still liked to see it. Now the fun, obviously, is working itself up to some sort of climax. And you want it damped down—literally. I wondered why." Charles Hardcastle had returned to his moody contemplation of the smoke-stained mist, and did not reply. "I don't dispute your wish," John went on. "I share it. But I still wonder why."

"I don't know." He turned, shrugged and began to walk back toward the house. "I can't give you a conscious reason for it, let alone a logical one. Therefore it is probably something which my conscious mind rejects as discreditable. Envy, perhaps? A feeling of being left out, and a consequent resentment? The basic human wish to cohere is as universal and powerful as gravity. That's why the thing has snowballed as it has. But I know I can't join the party. There's still that, you see—that's fundamental. Any more than you could. So I don't want it to be a success. Is that it, do you think?" He looked at John, genuinely troubled.

They went inside and started breakfast. John saw that there were only two places laid, and one of them was clearly his. He said, "I have met Father Freeman twice—met him properly, that is. Both times he left me shaken. He is clearly neither a simple crook nor a mountebank. Something comes through, and the urge to surrender is very strong. There is in consequence, when he is not there, an equally strong urge to run away from him. You say I couldn't join the party. I'm not sure that's true. Of me, I mean. Of you I feel sure it is. But I don't want to. And reason insists that I'm right. Therefore I am unwilling to put my reason at risk. Perhaps that's cowardice. Is it cowardice to have a proper appreciation of one's own weakness?"

Charles Hardcastle said, "Go on. You interest me profoundly. I hadn't understood that our attitudes were so fundamentally different."

"Cynthia understood from the start. She told me at a very early stage of our acquaintance that you were apt to regard me as a kindred soul—that wasn't what she said, exactly, but that was the gist of it—but that she wasn't at all sure I was. It's odd, isn't it? And the other day you told me that Cynthia could tell me more than you could about what Father Freeman was up to. You weren't mistaken in Cynthia. You wouldn't be, of course. But you were, in a way, mistaken about me, whereas Cynthia wasn't."

"But Cynthia couldn't join the party either. I'm certain of that. Aren't you?"

John said, "Cynthia, unlike you or me, is an innocent. She is armed at all points, and need neither surrender nor run away. So, in a very different sort of way, is Derek Potter."

Charles Hardcastle smiled at him. The smile lightened the atmosphere, so that they both decided simultaneously to have a second cup of coffee, and had to wave each other on politely over the coffee pot. "I dare you to tell him so," said Charles Hardcastle. "You try and see what you get."

John said cheerfully, "I know what I'd get. I've no intention of telling him so. But I'm right, all the same. He's a nice chap." A nice chap, he thought. God bless the law of usage. I know exactly what I want to say, and I have expressed it exactly and been exactly understood. Let the purists go chase themselves. Derek Potter is a nice chap.

"I'm glad," said Charles Hardcastle. "I mean, I'm glad you find him so. He's not easy, and I thought in your case the age gap would be just wrong."

"Cynthia spoke for me," said John. Mr. Hardcastle nodded with elaborate detachment and left it.

103

As he came into the bar of the Bell, John thought, "But I've seen this before," and then remembered where and when. Richard Garstin was draped against the bar, only this time no one talked at his elbow. Instead, George Curtis stood on the other side of the bar, watching him. No one spoke at all. The landlord's eyes shifted, as they had on that first dark evening, to take in John as he entered, and then went back to the man in front of him. Garstin did not seem to have heard John come in, but he jerked upright as suddenly as if a spring had been released inside him. He nodded to George Curtis and went out, passing John but not noticing him. He walked with quick, spasmodic movements, so that the image of a spring repeated itself in John's mind. A clockwork figure, moving because somebody at some time had stored this energy in him, and now it activated him without his choosing. George Curtis looked at him unhappily, half avoiding his eye. He said, "He doesn't say much, Mr. Garstin."

And is that an apology, thought John, or a disclaimer of knowledge? He said, "A nice man, though, you said, didn't you?"

"Oh, he's that. Or he was. I'm not sure, to tell the truth, he knows where he's going to properly half the time, not nowadays."

"He looks—I don't know—hard driven. Do you know what I mean?"

"Well, that's it, do you see? They're all after him. And all wanting something different. Or so I reckon. And he hasn't got it in him to take a line of his own. But I don't know, mind you. As I say, he doesn't say much."

"Can't he simply get out?"

"He ought to have, of course. But you've got to be fair. It would take some doing. You can see that, can't you? You're a younger man, of course. But you can see that, surely?"

104

"Yes," said John, "I can see that." He remembered the authority you did not question and the assurance that underlay it and flowed from it. He remembered Mrs. Garstin saying, "That's right," as she leaned forward to pour out the coffee. He remembered her saying, "Get in" as she opened the near-side door of her small black car. And at the back of his mind, all the time, was the image of the huge, solitary bed in the scented, almost empty room. There were bondages beyond all breaking. You had to be fair, even with clockwork automata who didn't say much.

George Curtis said, "But I don't like it. I don't like seeing him like that."

A car in the street outside started up and was put noisily into gear. Then it roared and was off like a rocket, heading westward for Upsindon. A voice across the street called out and was answered by another voice, and the two of them started to sing in lilting unison. For a moment there seemed nothing for it but to go away from Coyle now, while the going was good. But he could not do that, either. And tomorrow was the festival.

By early afternoon a small wind was blowing, and the sky sicklied over westward with a mounting haze. John walked out over the bridge, but today he was not going to Upsindon. Instead he took a lane that turned off right-handed uphill. He climbed steadily through the trees until he came out on to the top of the hills above the Gale. All he could see of Coyle was the unwanted top of St. Udan's tower, standing up now, still yellow, out of a pool of vapors. But the wind was colder here and even as he looked the color of the stone changed, and the familiar grayness fell over everything. Someone of the opposition, he thought, was working overtime. They would get their downpour yet. He turned eastward, following a track that ran between dry-stone walls thirty yards or so above the upward edge of the trees.

105

Somewhere along here there must be a road that led down to the back of Galehanger. A bit of a way around, Cynthia had said; but he did not know in which direction. It might, now he came to think of it, turn eastward and come out into the lane that ran between the wood and Tan Hill. In any case, it probably would not come as high as this. He must get down, at some point, into the trees; but for the moment he shrank from going downhill again. The moving air lightened the load on his mind, and he was unwilling to leave it.

In the end it was the track that made up his mind for him. It ended suddenly in two gates standing side by side across the width of it. Only a wall continued the line of the track, with a field on each side of it, each served by one of the gates. He went through the right-hand gate and followed the wall, still going eastward, until the land itself started to fall away and he saw the tops of trees in front. Now he knew where he was. Ahead of him was the eastward-facing slope of the hill, and below it, across the lane he had followed from the church, the saddle running out into the green cone of Tan Hill. He had passed right across the top of Coyle. If he was going to find his way back into it through the Gale, he must go back a bit and then turn down into the trees on the southern slope. He walked back to the twin gates and along the track until he came to the first gate on his left. He went through it and walked due south, making for the edge of the trees. The grass turned into a slope of bracken and furze, and below it, cut off from the upland pasture by a stiff barbed-wire fence, the trees stood darkly all along the side of the hill.

There was no gap in the fence as far as he could see in either direction. He went right-handed along it until he found a place where a sagging wire promised a reasonable chance of scrambling through without spiking himself or tearing his clothes. He crawled through gingerly, first his arms, then his head and

106

shoulders, then his lower half, one leg at a time. A barb on the bottom strand tugged momentarily at his trouser leg, but he lifted it clear. He slipped on the slope as his second leg came through, rolled a couple of yards and sat up among the trees of the Gale.

It was already surprisingly dark in the wood and, before he had gone very far, surprisingly quiet. The ground fell sharply between the great vertical columns of the standing timber. There was waist-high thicket everywhere, with a maze of green paths winding through it. It was Milk Wood all right. Given a certain amount of good will on all hands, there was unlimited privacy. The stolen embraces of generations had left an atmosphere of stealthy expectancy that brought him tiptoeing down through the trees, peering into the shadows and wondering what he would see next. What he saw was Cynthia, sitting, as he had first seen her, perched on a tree stump and staring at him, as he came down through the wood, with the eyes of a startled hare.

She unclasped her hands from around her knees and shot her feet to the ground, but did not move away from the stump. She stood there, half leaning back against it, with her feet together and her hands crossed over her breasts, still staring into his eyes as he came toward her as if she had never seen him before. He went up to her, breathless with a sort of compassionate exhilaration, and put his hands under her elbows, pulling her to him. Her hands stayed where they were between them, so that he felt the small sharp bones of her knuckles against his chest instead of the softness he had a right to expect.

Nature, by placing the prominent nose of humanity above its mouth, has made it necessary that lovers must turn their faces sideways when they kiss, one one way and one the other. The adjustment may with experience become instinctive, but it has at some point to be learned. Cynthia put her face up to be kissed, but left the disentangling of noses entirely to him, so that he had to turn his face almost horizontal to come at the expectant lips. He noted the fact with a small stab of pleasure before more serious business put it out of his mind. If she did not know much about kissing, she had more than the root of the matter in her. At some point her hands left their protective gesture and found their way around his neck as his closed around the small of her back. Having thus achieved a more traditional and satisfactory stance, they stood there in the dusk under the trees, pressed desperately against each other, while their mouths communicated what neither had yet attempted to put into words. Being experienced and instinct with longing, his hands began their explorations, and she, being innocent and utterly committed, did not stop them. But presently she took her mouth away from his and said, "I don't think—" and he said, "No, all right," and brought his hands firmly back to the tense muscles on each side of her spine.

A minute or two later she said, "But I love Dick Garstin." It was the first coherent statement either of them had made, and it was so obviously untrue that he felt justified in ignoring it. Having made this necessary gesture to the proprieties, she returned wholeheartedly to the business in hand. It was not, indeed, until the business threatened to get thoroughly out of hand that either of them spoke again. Then she said, "Darling, no," and pushed the engulfing male presence to a safer distance. John, breathless as if he had been swimming in rough water, said again, "No, all right," and stood there, at half-arm's length, looking down at her. The trees of the Gale, which had seen all this over and over again during their much more than human lifetime, sighed with gentle resignation, and for the moment the scene was played out.

Cynthia said, "I think we had better go down, don't you?" Never taking her eyes off his face, she straightened, without either coyness or confusion, the parts of her dress that had got themselves disarranged between the two of them. Then she held out her hand for his, and they walked so, hand in hand and quite silent, through the green maze of the wood until they came to the road that led to Galehanger. When they came to the edge of the trees, she stopped and turned to him. They kissed, quickly and lightly, once, dropped hands and walked, placidly and side by side, down the road, for all the world as if nothing had happened.

CHAPTER 12

"TONIGHT," said Charles Hardcastle, "we'll wander through the streets and note the qualities of people. If you agree, that is. I think myself it's a thing clearly not to be missed, whatever you feel about it. Hark at those bells. They'll have the tower down bell-ringing if they're not careful."

The bells had started soon after dawn and had stopped only for Communion at eight. Now they were off again, apparently ready to ring all day. Under the dark cloudwrack and this moving canopy of sound, Coyle waited for the evening. The excited preparations were all over. The singing had stopped. The people were about their proper jobs or indoors watching time pass. Only the bell-ringers, working in shifts, were on special duty. The wind of yesterday had gone, and the weather had ground to a halt. The night would be dark as pitch, but it was not going to rain.

John said, "Oh yes—I must see it, of course. They won't mind, will they?"

"On the contrary. We needn't disguise ourselves or anything. Nor need we join the procession. They won't all be processing, after all. Remember there was a bonfire on the tump long before Old Liberty came along. I imagine the rest of the village will go along and take up strategic positions on and near Tan Hill. The procession will start from the church and finish at the tump. Then they'll light the fire with proper ceremony, or someone will. And then the party really starts."

110

"Is there a time fixed?"

"The processionists are supposed to assemble at half past eight, I'm told. I get all this from Mrs. Mallett. She's a neutral, but all agog. I don't know how efficient it will all be. I should imagine quite efficient. I suppose they'll get away about nine."

The bells came to the end of their compulsive permutations and stopped. The silence was oppressive and absolute. Inside the stone walls there would be a roar of conversation. Faces were being mopped and dry throats slaked. It would be cheerful inside. But outside nothing showed. St. Udan's tower had said all it had to say for the moment and stood up silent in the damp gray light. The lancet windows of the ringers' chamber gave no more away than the louvers above them. Presently, if they had finished ringing for the time, there would be voices in the churchyard and feet on the flagstones, and the tower would confess its hidden manpower. But for the moment it might have done it all itself. No wonder, thought John, there were stories of bells that rang themselves. They were monstrous things to be at odds with.

He said, "I tell you what. I'll walk out to Tan Hill sometime today and spy out the land. I agree with you about the efficiency. I saw them building the fire. I should think they've got their dispositions pretty well cut and dried as well as the firewood. We may as well know what they are, don't you think?"

"Yes, well you do that. Then you can tell me what you think we'd better do this evening." Mr. Hardcastle paused and looked at John. "I haven't seen Cynthia this morning," he said. "Have you?"

"No. No, I was wondering where she was." He had not, in fact, seen her since they had walked in sedately from the wood to find Mr. Hardcastle looking at them speculatively from the door of the garage. "But I don't think she'll come with us this evening," he said.

"No? No, I suppose not." Mr. Hardcastle nodded and went

111

into the house. John, at odds with himself, went out through the white gate and down the steps. There were no voices in the churchyard, and as he passed the lych gate, the bells suddenly began again, driving him down Church Lane and through the empty village on a torrent of sound. There was no one anywhere, and he had a sudden apprehension that he and the bells were the only living things left in Coyle, and that they would have him, too, out of it if they could. They followed him down the street and under the eastern end of the churchyard. As he went up the valley they hovered over him, fainter here but still the only thing that moved. Tan Hill stood up against its backcloth of hanging woods, empty but waiting. The fire was a dark symmetrical apex to the green swell of the tump. All around the hill, fifteen yards or so below the fire, a ring of stakes had been driven into the turf and roped together. There was only one gap, straight above the point where the track from the lane reached the base of the hill. From there a line of steps led up to the fire, the treads cut level out of the chalk and the risers boarded and pegged to a strict vertical. It made the whole hill look artificial. Once, surely, there must have been just such a ceremonial way up the great mound of Silbury, so that whoever went up there could go with a dignity proper to the tremendous purposes that took them up. No one had built Tan Hill, but it did not need much adapting.

He looked everywhere, saw no one and began, with deliberate and conscious audacity, to climb the steps. The fire was walled all around with pine logs, so close together that they almost touched and laid at an angle of sixty degrees or more over a core of brushwood and a central mass of assorted kindling. Only at the top of the steps there was a gap in the logs giving access to the soft inflammable heart of the fire. Here, obviously, the ceremonial torch would be laid to the kindling, which by then, as Sheila Drew had said, would have been doped by the master hand of Elias Meadows. Paraffin, presumably. The whole fantastic preparation did not, as he knew, preclude the most prosaic efficiency. The thing would burn all right. And then the party would start. That was Charles Hardcastle, the inveterately profane, speaking from his ringside seat. He clung to Charles Hardcastle's profanity as a dreamer clings, in the worst throes of nightmare, to the conviction that he is in fact dreaming and need only wake himself to disperse the horror threatening him.

Once more, from the top of the tump, he looked all around him. Even up here the dark woods of the Gale hung over him. He could see nobody, but he felt himself overlooked and did not like it. He went down the steps again, and found that they were a lot less easy to negotiate going down. He had almost reached the lane when he noticed that the bells had stopped, but he could not say when. In the lane he turned right, making for the saddle between Tan Hill and the woods. Somewhere along here, if he was right, the Galehanger drive must open on to the lane, but he did not think he would take it. He found it, in fact, a hundred yards farther on, where the lane dipped again on the far side of the saddle. But he did not want to go back to Coyle yet. Coyle this evening required his presence, but for the moment all he wanted was to get clear of it. Over his shoulder the bells began again, and he hurried on, not hoping to lose them, but wanting if he could to dull their insistence by putting a reasonable space between himself and them. He did not get back to Coyle till nearly six, and by then the bells had stopped.

Charles Hardcastle greeted him with a sort of morose jocularity. As he had expected, it got dark early. The village below crawled with small moving lights, but they could hear nothing. At about half past seven Cynthia appeared suddenly from upstairs, muffled from head to heel. John, sprawled uneasily in a long chair, scrambled to his feet, and they looked at each other long and silently. She gave him the ghost of a smile, which re-

113

newed his assurance of her, but increased his inarticulate disquiet. He had seen candidates smile at each other like that on the steps of the Examination Schools, recognizing each other's distress, but muffled from each other in the private experience of a common apprehension. Then she nodded and went out. He did not see her again that night.

He and his host drank more than their usual ration of whiskey and ate the cold meal Mrs. Mallet had left them. Sometime after eight they roused themselves with a simultaneous inability to sit still any longer. Charles Hardcastle said, "I think the thing to do is to go out by the drive. It's dark, but I'll take a torch. That will bring us out under Tan Hill, and then we can see what the rest of the world is doing. Unless you want to go through the village, that is."

"No, no. Let's go by the wood, certainly. I don't know whether the *profanum vulgus* is allowed on the hill. The fire itself is roped off, but I imagine the processionists will want to be there or thereabouts. I don't know whether you'll get your ringside seat tonight."

"I'm not sure I want one. But we'll see."

They put on coats and went out on to the terrace. Coyle was still quiet, but looked like a nest of fireflies. Charles Hardcastle surveyed it in silence. "I hope he knows what he's doing," he said. Then they turned and made for the back of the house. Even with the torch picking out the road, their eyes stretched themselves to the darkness of the wood, and when they came out into the lane they were surprised by the unexpected visibility. They stood listening to the murmur that filled the silence and then, as they went right-handed up the slope of the saddle, saw that the lower slopes of the hill were full of people. They stood in groups or sat huddled on the turf, waiting. There was a faint stir and rustle of whispered conversation, but mostly they were silent. It was all immensely solemn.

114

John said, "I reckon we can go up a bit." He said it in a whisper, and Charles Hardcastle nodded. They picked their way up between the silent groups, aiming always for where the black cone of the fire stood up against the lowering starless sky. When they got close to the ropes, John moved across the slope until the gap in the ring and the bottom of the ceremonial steps were just above them. There they stopped to wait. No one was right against the ropes. There was a band of empty turf several yards deep outside them. There, he felt sure, the processionists would take up their places, and the waiting crowd would then press in behind them, until the fire, beyond its protective girdle, was ringed by a mass of people. Only at one point would the ring be broken to admit the one person who had to enter it; and there the steps would be ready to conduct him to the top. From along the valley the clock of St. Udan's struck nine. There was a moment's dead silence in the waiting crowd, and then a wordless murmur of excitement. The sky over Coyle glowed suddenly, then faded, then glowed again, this time with an orange fiery light caught and reflected on the underside of swirling clouds of smoke. The torches had been lit and were already on the move.

It seemed a long time before they heard the singing, but it could not really have been very long. It was the children's voices they heard first, and when these left off singing there was silence altogether. But presently the deeper voices made themselves heard, and from then on the thing was continuous, though with different voices in command at different times. The glow in the sky brightened until the dark shoulder of the hanging wood showed clearly against it. Then two twinkling points of light appeared suddenly, lower than they had been looked for, and the crowd on the hill muttered and swayed on its feet. A second pair of torches followed the first, and two by two the long crocodile of moving lights crept slowly around

115

the corner of the hill. The smoke in the still air rolled sluggishly above it, and the red light and the singing voices went up continuously under the rolling smoke. John, his apprehension forgotten and helpless now in the grip of an enormous excitement, waited for them to come.

The leading torches reached the gate at the bottom of the hill, paused for a moment and then turned into the gate. There were torches now all the way back to the bend where the lane came around under the Gale, and there were still more coming. He made fumbling attempts to count them but his counting always broke down because he shifted his eyes back to look at the head of the procession. They came on, unhurried but unhesitating, not marching, nor, he could see now, even very carefully ranged, but moving steadily. There was no straggling. The whole monstrous column moved of a piece, as if it was in fact a kind of creature with an organic life of its own. It felt its way through the gate and crept slowly in a long spiral around the smooth cone of the hill. Tan Hill was alight everywhere now except at the top, where the level platform of the tump threw its shadow over the waiting pile of the fire.

The processionists came in groups, led by the Friendly Girls, but there was no ribaldry now from the crowd that parted to let them through and then closed in behind them. They held their torches high and walked with eyes wide open under them, utterly absorbed in what they were doing. All around the hill the procession went, closing in on the line of stakes until the head of the column came to the gap at the foot of the steps. There it halted, and the long tail came slowly up from the lane, wrapping itself around itself, until the torches were five deep in places all around the ring of ropes and there were no more to come. There was a surge of movement all around him, and John found himself, almost running, borne on the wave of people that closed in from below and behind it on the great ring of light.

116

He pushed his way shamelessly to the gap in the ring and felt the pressure of bodies build up behind him, until nobody moved, or could move, any more. Nothing moved now but the dancing flames and the billowing smoke above them. The air was foul with the smell of burning pitch, but still the processionists, standing to the ropes and holding their torches high above them, sang as if their lives depended on it. They sang like this, standing still and looking up, for another minute or more, and then stopped altogether. He looked around the ring and saw that here and there the torches were beginning to die down, though they were still held high above the crowded heads. Then a flicker of movement caught his eye, and he found Mrs. Garstin almost beside him. She stood in the gap, staring up the steps which ran up in front of her. Father Freeman stood close behind her. He stood, almost for the first time that John had seen him, straight up, and towered over her. He held a small unlit torch in his left hand and, as John watched him, fumbled in a pocket under his cassock and produced a box of matches. The whole thing was extraordinarily deliberate and prosaic. Stage illusion on the grand scale suddenly yielded to a glimpse of stage management; and as John's excitement collapsed, his apprehension came back like a cold weight at the pit of his stomach. The vicar struck a match and held it to the head of the torch. It spluttered for a moment and then caught. He held it steady until it was properly afire. Then he touched Mrs. Garstin's arm and, as she half turned, handed her the torch. She nodded and took it. Both faces, in the red, flickering light, seemed completely expressionless. Father Freeman motioned her on with his hand and then, when she did not move, seemed to push her gently toward the bottom step. She nodded again, still with the same sleepwalker's incomprehension. Then, holding the torch high above her, delicate, expressionless, exquisite in the moving light and the dead silence that surrounded her, she began to go slowly up the steps.

117

She looked unbelievably small moving alone into the center of that expectant ring of fire. Anything less like the lady of the manor opening the church bazaar John had never seen. To his eyes she looked more like the priestess of some much older and less respectable ceremony. Or the victim, he thought, racked again with his intolerable anxiety. Both perhaps, the priestess-victim. Whatever she was, she was alone, and Coyle, packed tight against the ropes all around, watched her breathlessly. She was nearly at the top now. For a moment she seemed to hesitate. Then, with the same exquisite, unhurried motion, she went up and stood on the top step. She stood there, holding her torch high above her, and seemed half to turn as though to look back to the bottom of the steps, where Father Freeman stood like a pillar of darkness, willing her on. Then she turned back to the pile and, bringing her torch down in a slow arc of fire, laid it to the brushwood at her feet. There was a crackle as the flames took immediate hold, and then at John's elbow the vicar caught his breath suddenly and stumbled forward shouting. "Down!" he shouted. "Down! Come down, Mary! For God's sake, come down!"

CHAPTER 13

WIDE-EYED and open-mouthed, the village growled in its throat
and surged forward against the rope. At the top of the steps,
outlined against the flames of the burning brushwood, Mrs. Garstin half turned, stepped back, missed her footing on the edge of
the step and fell. She fell sideways on to the turf and rolled twice
over down the slope before her clutching hands checked her
fall. It was the fall that saved her. Over the murmur of the
crowd another voice spoke suddenly, as if a very large giant
had coughed deep in his throat, and an enormous surge of
orange flame poured out from the heart of the fire. It poured out
horizontally, breaking out on every side from between the
logs, but reaching out one prodigious arm of fire from the gap
and across the place where, only a second before, Mrs. Garstin
had been standing. It passed a yard above her as she lay on the
turf slope and then turned upward, merging itself into the
huge vertical column of flame that roared up from the fire.

It was all over in a second. There was a further second of utter
silence, and then everyone shouted at once. John was aware of
the vicar, motionless in front of him with his hands still raised
as if to pull Mrs. Garstin back. Then he dodged around the tall
figure and was racing up the slope. He flung himself down on
his knees and gathered Mrs. Garstin into his arms. Her eyes were
open and staring. She had dropped her torch in her fall, and
with her empty right hand she crossed herself spasmodically

119

and repeatedly. "Mother of God," she said. "Mother of God." She was untouched by the flame. He got an arm under her shoulders and jerked her half on to her feet. The fire roared above them, but its whole fury went upward and here there was no more than a tolerable radiated heat. With the slope helping him, half carrying and half dragging her, he began to get her down the hill. Then Father Freeman was with them and half a dozen more. There was bedlam now all around the hill, and there was nothing more he could do. He left her to the others and walked, alone in the orange light of the fire, down the steps to the gap in the fence. He pushed his way through the surge of staring faces. Only he wanted to go down and there was always a body ready to move upward into his place. Quite suddenly he found himself alone, behind the last of the hypnotized backs and, under their shadow, in comparative darkness. He walked quickly down the hill and then, as the slope eased and the going got easier, started to run. He ran down through the gate and out into the lane. Out of breath now, he dropped to a walk as the lane climbed the saddle, but on the far side broke into a run again. He did not know where he was running, but the urge to get away was irresistible. He had never found out where this lane did go to, but it went away from Coyle. A bend in the lane put a tree-clad shoulder of the hill between him and the distant glow of the fire, and in the soft darkness he dropped to a walk again. He walked furiously until he saw lights ahead and came to a pub on the left-hand side of the road. The hill had flattened out here, and there were no more trees. From what he could see, the land behind the pub ran up gently in pasture and arable land to a humped skyline. There was no village, only the pub with a gravel pull-in for cars in front of it. He did not know how long he had been walking. There were lights on the ground floor, but no one about and no cars.

The door was shut but not locked. He pushed it open and

went into an empty bar. A man in shirt sleeves came through a door behind the bar and looked at him with a sort of apologetic apprehension. John said, "Am I too late? I'm afraid I don't know what time it is."

"Oh, I'm afraid you are. Gone eleven, it has. Matter of fact, I just opened the door again because there's a gentleman staying and he'll be coming in presently." He looked at John, so that John wondered whether he showed any mark of what he had come through. But he could not think what it could be. The landlord said, "I could give you a soft drink, if you'd like one. Come far, have you?"

That was it, of course. The pub was in the middle of nowhere, and he had appeared suddenly and without a car. People did not travel on foot nowadays without explanation. John said, "I'd like one very much if you can manage it. Lemon or something. Not fizzy. Just with water."

The landlord nodded and got him what he wanted. He said, "Are you going on to Coyle? It's quite a step."

John said, "No." He took a long pull at the sourish stuff and felt better. "No," he said, "that's where I've come from." It occurred to him as he said it that he had to go back to Coyle, but it did not seem worth elaborating the thing.

The landlord said, "They'll have had their bonfire there tonight. Always do on the tenth."

"That's right. They were starting as I left. They had a procession. Very pretty, it was." He paid for his drink and took his change. "Well," he said, "I must be getting on." He was suddenly frightened that the landlord would ask him where he was going, and he did not know the answer. He made for the door. "Good night," he said. "Thank you for the drink. I needed it."

The landlord said, "Good night," and watched him out of the door. It was surprisingly dark outside. He set out back the way he had come, and knew at once that he was very tired.

"Very pretty, it was," he said to the darkness. "Well, all right, so it was. Very pretty indeed, up to a point." He had avoided coherent thought on the way out, and now that his mind was more settled, he was too tired to do any good with it. He let his mind go blank and concentrated on his walking.

The hillside grew steeper on his right, and presently the trees began. He saw the lights of the car coming toward him from some way off. He turned off the road, plunged blind through a shallow ditch and stood in the shadow while the car went past. He did not notice it particularly. The gentleman who was staying, perhaps. He scrambled out on to the road again, and wondered as he did so why he had got himself out of the car's lights. It was symptomatic of his state of mind, he decided, but not logical. He did not want anybody to ask him any more questions tonight. He did not know the answers, and he was too tired to think of them. He hoped George Curtis would have gone to bed, so long as he had left the side door open. He'd do that, surely. He walked on, disturbed by the interminable length of the road he had come out over so quickly. He wondered at times whether Coyle was on this road, or even existed at all. It was not until the road began to climb sharply under him that he knew he had come to the saddle and had Tan Hill on his left.

There was no fire on the tump now. There wouldn't be, of course. Burning the way it was going, it would have burned itself out long ago. The ashes would still be hot, but that was all there would be, only ashes. When he got to the top of the rise, he stopped and looked across the fence to his left. The outline of the hill was just visible, and as he looked a faint glow showed for a moment on top and then went again. That would be the ashes of the fire, mostly black now, but responding to any slight movement in the damp air on top of the hill. He found a negotiable gap, scrambled through it and started to walk down the slight slope where the saddle dipped toward the base of the hill. It was all completely quiet. Whatever had happened after he had left, it was all over and everyone had gone home. He came to the foot of the hill and started to climb. The turf was trampled and very slippery, and he went slowly.

He stopped with a jerk as something loomed up in front of him, and then realized it was one of the stakes that carried the ropes. The rope was still there, but hanging loose, and the next stake was down. The rope at some point had gone down before the crowd, but that would have happened anyway. Once the fire was going, the people weren't going to keep their distance. That was when the party was due to start. He went on up, going cautiously foot by foot until he was nearly under the tump. Then a puff of air came sluggishly from the direction of Coyle. The ashes on the top of the mound glowed again, and he saw, only for a moment but quite clearly, a figure moving across the glow. There was no detail, and the curve of the mound hid all but the top of it. But there was someone there, up on top of the tump, moving close against the ashes of the dead fire. He dropped to his knees on the damp scarred turf and crouched there, straining his eyes toward the almost invisible outline above him, and willing the sluggish air to produce enough movement to rouse the ashes again.

For a minute or more nothing happened and then he heard the noise. It was regular and systematic, but so faint and indefinite that it did not suggest any clear picture to his mind. But it was a man-made noise, not a natural one. Somebody was doing something up by the fire, doing it softly and regularly, but he could not tell what. He rose on his knees, craning over the curve of the chalk in case there might be anything to see. The noise suddenly defined itself more clearly as the faintest possible clink, as if metal, very cautiously, had touched metal. Then for a moment it stopped altogether. Nothing came to his ears now, and

123

still the wind did not come to rouse the ashes. He let himself down gradually into his former crouch, and was aware that the regular noise had started again. It went on for perhaps half a minute. Then he half heard, or wholly imagined, another clink. If he heard it at all, it was even fainter than the first, but again the regular noise had stopped.

He rose on his knees again, and felt the air moving very gently on his right cheek. It was so slight a movement that he thought nothing would come of it, but as he stared up into the darkness a small surge of soft air went past him, and for the fraction of a second the ashes glowed red on top of the mound. The figure was turned half sideways with its back to him. It was stooped over the remains of the fire, reaching forward with something long, a stick or a length of metal. He could still see no more than the top half of it. It was quite unidentifiable. Whoever it was, they were moving the thing they held systematically backward and forward. An association of ideas brought Elias Meadows back to him, Elias Meadows and his long stick. The leech-gatherer, he had thought, with his long gray staff of shaven wood, stirring the water of the moorish flood and looking for leeches.

That was it. He had got it now. Whoever it was up there was stirring over the ashes of the fire, looking for something. And it had to be metal of a sort, or it would not have survived the heat. Something, something very small but metallic, probably several of them, had been left in the almost dead heart of the fire. And someone knew they were there, and did not want them left there, and had come to find them if he could. John began to lower himself on to the turf slope again. He was halfway down when his left foot slipped and went back behind him. He did not fall, but his hands came down on to the turf with the faintest possible thud, and he knew, though he had not heard it, that his foot must have made a scuffling sound as it slipped. He crouched almost flat on the turf, not daring to look up. He was suddenly very much afraid. He was afraid of whoever it was up above him in the darkness, with a long piece of metal in his hands, intent on his private business and not wishing to be disturbed.

For what seemed a very long time nothing happened at all. If only whoever it was would go back to his raking through the ashes, John thought, he could feel reasonably certain that he had not given himself away. But the regular repetitive noise he had first heard never came again. He crouched there, mouth open, eyes staring in the darkness, ready to scramble to his feet and run at the first sign of movement in his direction. Then he heard, very faintly but unmistakably, in the same soft clink of metal against metal he had heard before. It was repeated almost immediately, and then repeated a second time. Then the silence shut down again, and this time nothing came to break it. The chill from the wet turf struck up through his knees and hands, and he shivered suddenly and uncontrollably. It's all right for you, you bastard, he thought, you've got the remains of the fire to keep you warm. Do something, can't you? Make a movement of some sort. He shivered again, and still, up there on top of the mound, nothing happened and no one moved.

He knew if he stayed where he was much longer, he would be almost incapable of moving, certainly of moving with speed, if he had to. The thing could not go on. Then the one thing he was not waiting for happened. A breeze blew suddenly along the banked trees of the Gale, touched him with a cold finger as he crouched shivering on the chalk and, a moment later, blew the ashes of the fire up into a bright red glow. The outline of the mound stood out black against it, but nothing else was visible. He raised himself, shaking, on his knees and still saw nothing. Then, stiff and unsteady, he got first one foot and then the other to the ground and began to creep up the remaining slope. Still the breeze held and still the fire glowed red, and suddenly his head came over the convex curve of the tump, and he saw the whole glowing circle of ash and the flat space all around it. There was nothing there. No figure, no rake, no metal something for the rake to sound against. Someone had been there, and raked the ashes over, and found whatever he was looking for and gathered them up. But whoever it was had gone and taken his finds with him.

He turned and went quickly down the slope toward the saddle. The way he had come was the safest way to go, and there was nothing more he could do on the tump, not with the fire still glowing as it was. He went as quietly as he could, but was concerned mainly to keep moving. He felt deadly cold and slightly light-headed, but was no longer conscious of being tired. He crossed the dip, hurried up the far side, found his gap in the fence and scrambled through into the lane. He thought for a moment of turning back and following the Galchanger drive through the wood, but the idea of that pitch darkness with no torch to help him was more than he could stomach. It was dark enough in the lane, but at least he could see the road before and behind him. Going warily, but making what speed he could, he set out for Coyle.

He saw and heard nothing all the way, and when he came round under the churchyard wall and into the end of the street, all Coyle was abed. In two upper windows he saw the faint amber glow of a nightlight, and pictured a child, or perhaps two children in a bed, sleeping fitfully after the excitements of the evening. But everything else was dark. Whether there had been panic and disaster after he had left, or the near-orgy of George Curtis's melancholy imagination, Coyle was sleeping it off. The festival was over, the bonfire was out. St. Udan's tower, still under sentence of death, had another year to face; and whatever else had happened, he found it impossible to believe that Mary Garstin had signed its reprieve.

Well past the proper limit of nervous exhaustion, John now

126

felt restless and wide awake. If the side door of the Bell was open, he could get to bed any time. If it was shut, he was out for the night anyhow; he would never in any case try to rouse George Curtis to let him in. He turned up Church Lane and stood for a moment at the lych gate, looking up at the tower. He would not have been surprised if Father Freeman was up there, wrestling with whatever it was he wrestled with on the dark platform above the slowly crumbling masonry. But nothing, nothing in the world, would have induced him to go up and see. He looked up at Galehanger, in the faint hope of seeing a light showing. He had lost Charles Hardcastle in the sudden surge to the ropes and had not seen him since. He could have done, now, with a whiff of his sturdy profanity and even more with two good fingers of his whiskey; but Charles Hardcastle, as was only to be expected, was in bed. He did not know where Cynthia had been or was, but he hoped she was in bed too. A sudden warmth touched his chilled mind. He wished her good-night, and turned back for the Bell.

The side door was open, and as he came in, the door from the kitchen opened and George Curtis put his head out. He said, "Would you like a cup of tea?" He looked John over and added, "I'd say put something in it, if I were you." John said, "Oh, yes please." He gulped down the black brew made supremely comforting with a solid slug of Scotch at the bottom of it. He felt immediately better, and a moment later overpoweringly sleepy. George Curtis said, "I was wondering where you'd got to," but it was a genuine statement, not a question, and John did not answer it. "I heard it went off all right," said George Curtis. "They tell me the fire caught a bit quick and Mrs. Garstin had a bit of a fall, but it went off all right."

John opened his half-closed eyes and looked at the perfectly serious face in front of him. "Oh yes," he said, "it went off all right." He said good-night and went upstairs to bed.

CHAPTER 14

"I LOST YOU," said Charles Hardcastle. "I was watching the tail end of the procession come in. I was fascinated by the way they fitted themselves along the ropes. Then there was a rush to get in behind them, which I wasn't keen to do myself, so I hung back. By that time you'd gone. I imagined you must be up front somewhere. Where were you? In with the Girls' Friendly?"

"Not that I know of. I was close to the gangway. If you call it that. The gap in the rope, anyway. When did the vicar and Mrs. Garstin come? With the procession? I just found them there suddenly."

"Ah. No, that I can tell you. The vicar came at the end of the procession. If he'd had a torch, he'd have looked for all the world like a walking lighthouse. Well, he had one, I think, but it wasn't lit. Anyway, he waited by the gate into the lane, and a moment later Mrs. Garstin drove up in her own car. She left it in the lane, and Old Liberty escorted her up the hill. They vanished into the back of the crowd, and after that I couldn't see what happened. If I'd thought of it, I'd have gone further down the hill. I could see the tump from there. As it was, all I could see was the lights and the backs of the people in front of me. There was a tremendous flare as the fire caught, and everybody shouted. There's some story of Mary Garstin's falling down the steps or something. Did you see what happened? All I

know is that after the fire was well started I saw Old Liberty taking her down the hill to her car again. But I was further round
the hill by then, and I didn't get a close view of them. They were
halfway down before I noticed them, anyway."

John filled his pipe with tremendous and unnecessary concentration. When he looked up, he was, for better or worse,
committed. He said, "She lit the fire, yes, and there was a bit of
a blow-back. She stepped back and got her foot over the edge of
the step. Or that was what it looked like. At any rate, she
slipped and came down. The vicar and I ran and helped her up.
She was all right, I think. Anyway, the vicar took her over. I left
soon after that. What happened after they'd gone?"

Charles Hardcastle shook his head. "I didn't stay much longer
myself. They started singing again round the fire, and after that
I imagine there was general merry-making. I went home to bed."
He paused, frowning. "I don't know, I get the impression it
didn't really go according to plan, but no one is going to say so.
If Coyle wants to shut up, clams aren't in the same class. I
wondered if in fact they hadn't found the traditional junketing
more fun without Old Liberty's trimmings, but couldn't say so.
Have you talked to anyone?"

"Only George Curtis when I got in. And he wasn't there. He
said he gathered it went off all right. He didn't say who'd told
him so."

"Oh—Mrs. Curtis, obviously. She'd have been in the procession for sure. But of course, she's one of the faithful. If she says
everything went off all right, you can take it that's the official
version. And you won't shake it."

John nodded. He said, "Is Cynthia around?"

"I haven't seen her this morning, no. I fancy she's still in
bed. I don't know what time she got in, of course."

"She wasn't—she didn't take part in the procession, did she?"

"No." He said it quite decisively, and John was suddenly

129

aware of an agonized parental concern under the mask of elaborate detachment. He wondered how much of Cynthia's movements Charles Hardcastle made it his business, in fact, to know about. He said, "I don't think you need worry about her, you know. Is that a fearful impertinence?"

Charles Hardcastle looked at him with careful, kindly attention. "You speak with some authority," he said. "It's not an impertinence, no. Only—you have good ground for what you say?"

"I believe I have, yes. You don't mind?"

"My dear chap, I'm delighted. It is my affectation to be the detached observer. But I have not liked all I have observed. I think you know that. I welcomed you as, at least, a catalyst."

"And I told you I was not exactly doing you a favor."

"So you did, yes. And I accepted that. But I still welcomed you. It was not for me, in this day and age, to ask you your intentions."

John laughed. "I have already been asked that. By Derek Potter."

"Derek? Good Lord. I told you he was a nice chap. But how little one knows. Wait till you're a mere parent."

They parted with a large, inarticulate friendliness, and John, suddenly very old and solemn, went down the steps and out into the village street. He paused, saw no one about and turned left. To hell with mysteries, he thought. I have only one main concern. But I must know. He walked down under the eastern end of the churchyard and set out for Tan Hill.

There was still no sunlight, but the valley was full of clear white daylight, and the oppression of the night lifted as he walked. He walked boldly up the lane, turned in at the gate and started to climb the hill. The woods hung silent above him, but were empty of menace. He could do what he had to do, and because he did not mind whether anyone was watching him or not, no one watched him.

The fire was an almost perfect circle of dead gray ash, crusted now where the damp had settled on it as it cooled. To his eyes, because he knew what he knew, it was unnaturally flat and regular, but to the casual eye nothing would show. He found, on the outer edge of the circle, a short length of charred but solid wood and set to work. He could not kneel in the black mess, but he squatted in it, aware, as he did so, that the convex curve of the tump hid him from any observer in the road below. Only someone up in the Gale could have seen what he was at, and he felt a solid, wholly unreasonable assurance that there was no one there.

If, as he thought probable, he had disturbed the nocturnal searcher, he might not have finished the job. There might still be something left worth looking for. At any rate, it was worth trying. He crouched on his heels on the empty hilltop, scratching busily among the soft debris of the fire. Metal was the key. Whatever he was looking for, it was metal. He wished he had, like his predecessor, a metal tool to work with, but he had nothing but a knife with a blade much too short for the job. Three times his stick struck something hard, but turned up only a calcined pebble. Five minutes later an unmistakably metallic ring set him scrabbling among the ash with his fingers. He brought up a five-inch nail, bent to a right angle and crusted and pitted with orange rust. He sat back on his heels, turning it over in his hands and trying to give it a reasonable significance. Old timber, once cut and used, was full of rusty nails. Fencing posts, doorposts, roof timbers, excellent firing once they were broken and out of use, and all stuck with old nails nobody would bother to pull out. The head of the nail, now he looked at it closely, was much more corroded than the point, as if it had been long exposed to the weather before ever it got into the fire. It was an old nail, almost certainly. He dropped it, rust and all, into his pocket and went on with his scratching.

131

He turned up two more nails, a piece of metal strapping with the remains of a nail driven through it, a coil of wire, a section of hinge, and then, almost in the center of the circle, a tight ring or collar of flat metal, half fused with the heat of the fire, which he could not identify. He searched laboriously and with increasing irritation, but found nothing else. He sighed, straightened his cramped legs and picked his way to the bare, scorched chalk at the edge of the fire. He took his filthy trophies from his pocket and threw them down together on the turf. They clinked softly against each other, and he was reminded instantly of the noises he had heard from his hiding place halfway down the side of the tump. He could see now what whoever it was had done. He had raked through the ashes with some sort of metal rake, stopped raking when he struck metal and pulled what he had found out to the edge of the fire. Then, just before he had gone, he had put his collection together and bundled it up, probably in a bag or handkerchief if it was still too hot for his pocket. Anything he had not wanted he had no doubt dropped back into the ashes, including probably the nails. Then he had gone, either satisfied with his job or in haste because he suspected he was not alone on his hilltop and the glowing fire was too bright for his liking. John sighed again and with more determination than hope dropped his finds back again into his pocket. Then he started to go down the hill.

There was still no one about. He walked slowly, trying to recapture in detail the stupefying moment when the fire had exploded. There had been no sharp report, only that deep sudden cough. It was not explosives in the ordinary sense he had to reckon with, only an instantaneous and violent combustion. Petrol was the obvious answer, but how to store petrol in the heart of the pile without leaving recognizable containers? Whatever had been collected from the ashes afterward, it was nothing like cans or drums. Something much smaller than that. Something

132

that would not be noticed as the fire burned down and could be collected, if at all, later and at leisure.

He took his finds one by one out of his pocket, considering them as he walked and then, when he could not make them fit in any way the idea he had in mind, throwing them aside into the hedge. He did this until he had only the metal collar left. This he could not dismiss, because he could not identify it or attribute any purpose to it. Just before he reached the village he stopped and sat down at the side of the lane. He took out his knife and began to scratch at the orange coagulate that stood up on one side of the collar like the bezel on a ring. It came away reluctantly in granular flakes, revealing nothing. Then a larger lump broke off suddenly, and he said, "Ah!" and sat there, with the knife in one hand and the collar in the other, staring at what he had uncovered. It was heavily oxidized and had lost its sharp edges, but it could be only one thing. It was the slotted head of a screw. The shank of the screw was lost in the general corrosion, but it must lie tangentially along the side of the collar. He said, "Ah" again, folded the blade of the knife against the edge of the tarmac and dropped the knife in his pocket. He took the collar in both hands now and turned it over and over, looking at it from every angle, until he made it, charred and shapeless as it was, fit decisively the picture he had in his mind. He had no doubt now. It was a small hose-clip. It must have been screwed up to give almost the maximum compression to whatever it was it had been required to compress. Unless he was mistaken, it had been one of several. Several clips, all screwed up tight on the soft stuff, whatever it was, they had been fitted around. The stuff had gone, irrecoverably transmuted in the orange column of fire, and only the clips had been left. And of those all but one had been gathered up and taken away by the person who had put them there, and only one was left. This he had, and it gave him, unless he was mistaken, part of the answer. But he did not

133

know the rest. He got up, dropped the clip back into his pocket and walked on into the village.

He said to George Curtis, "What time did Mrs. Garstin come in from Upsindon yesterday evening?"

"Mrs. Garstin? She came through about twenty past nine."

"Was Mr. Garstin with her?"

"Mr. Garstin?" He shook his head, never taking his eyes off John's face. "Mr. Garstin was in Frantham yesterday evening. He came in here about eight. He was on his way then. He wasn't here at all, not after that."

"Did he have Miss Drew with him?"

"Here? He wouldn't have her with him here."

"No? No, I suppose not." A sudden wave of anger engulfed him. Damn them all, he thought. Let them burn each other with their fool fire festivals if they want to. What business is it of mine? But there were still things he wanted to know, and things he could not ask, and things he could ask but dare not. He said, "Was Mrs. Curtis with the procession?"

George Curtis was as watchful as ever, but there was an indefinable air of relief about him. He even smiled slightly. "Oh yes," he said. "She wouldn't miss it, not with its being Father Freeman's idea."

"What did she tell you about it?"

"About what?" The moment of lightness had passed, and all the barriers were up again.

"Well—about the fire." He took a breath and went straight ahead. "About Mrs. Garstin's accident."

"Mrs. Garstin's accident?" This was too elaborate altogether. For all his palpable anxiety, George Curtis had the simple man's natural incapacity as a prevaricator. But he held his ground. "Well," he said, "she didn't say much about it. Just that she went to light the fire, and it burnt up a bit fierce, and she stepped back and came down over the step. Something of that

134

sort. But she wasn't hurt."

"Did she know Mrs. Garstin was going to light the fire? I mean—was that part of the program?"

For a fraction of a second George Curtis stared at him with something very like hostility. Then he spoke with a curious deliberation and emphasis. He said, "No one knew she was going to light it. They all thought the vicar was. It was a surprise when Mrs. Garstin came."

Brought up short by a fresh and unexpected permutation of possibilities, John stared back at him, and for a moment neither of them said anything. Then George Curtis said, "You been up the tump?"

It was John's turn to prevaricate, but he knew he could not and was not sure he wished to. "Yes," he said, "just now." He waited, daring the little man to go further, but George Curtis only nodded. Then, suddenly and disconcertingly, he smiled, shrugged slightly and turned away. "I've got my business to attend to," he said.

Too preoccupied to worry over moral defeat, John too turned and went upstairs to his room. He still liked George Curtis and did not grudge him the last word. He took the hose-clip out of his pocket, looked around vaguely for somewhere to put it and finally dropped it into a small drawer in the massive mahogany dressing table. Then he went downstairs and out into the yard. The car had its hood up, and for all the mild air he did not feel inclined to lower it. The instinct to travel alone was very strong. The car was immediately identifiable, but he felt happier in the semi-invisibility under the canvas roof. He backed and turned her, nosed cautiously out into the street and turned left for Upsindon.

The lodge gates were open, but there was no one about. He went up the drive, left the car in the gravel sweep and went up the beautiful steps to the door. The maid who answered his ring

135

was obviously local talent. She was neat but had none of the professional domestic's manner.

"I'm afraid Mrs. Garstin isn't very well," she said. "I could ask—"

"No," said John. "No, don't worry her. Is Mr. Derek in, do you know?"

"I'm afraid he went out. But he'll be back for lunch. Perhaps if you could come this afternoon—"

"Yes, all right. I'll do that. Thank you."

He got back into the car and sat there thinking. Mrs. Garstin was not very well, but he knew with absolute certainty that there was nothing wrong with her physically. She was not a woman who would ever be ill. Mental distress there would be, and he wished he knew of what sort. He remembered the staring eyes and the distraught repetitive imprecation. But there was nothing he could do here.

He drove slowly back to the village and into the Bell yard. He did not want to see George Curtis again and went straight to his room. He wandered over to the window and stood there, looking out. The tower looked back at him, and for the first time he hated the sight of it and wished it down. There would be no peace in Coyle so long as it stood. Oh, whistle me up a wind, he thought. That was what was wanted. A clean, tearing gale, that would blow the cloud-roof off the valley and bring the bedeviled tower down harmlessly in the churchyard, where only the dead were.

He turned to go downstairs and then, on an impulse, went to the dressing table and opened the small top drawer. It was almost with relief that he found it empty. The clip had gone, and he did not very much mind where.

CHAPTER 15

DEREK POTTER SAID, "Hullo. Did you want to see my mother? I gathered you did."

"I should like to, if she's feeling up to it. How is she?"

"I haven't seen her. I don't think there's anything wrong physically. There's been no doctor or anything. I gather she's upset. The vicar's been in and out. Whether that has done good or harm I can't say." He stopped and looked at John with a touch of uncertainty. "She can get upset, you know. I mean—I think I may have given you the impression of a tough character. Well—so she is in some ways. But she is vulnerable in others. There are areas of great uncertainty in her mind. Only they don't fit the general picture, and you may well not have noticed them."

"Yes," said John, "I have had glimpses, I think. More than one."

"And the trouble is, the vicar plainly knows where the gaps in her defenses are. Or one gap, anyway."

"The hidden spring, you said."

"Did I? Well, that's near enough. Yes, I remember now. I said if I knew what hidden spring he touched, I'd have a go at it myself. But I didn't, and I still don't. What happened yesterday?"

John found himself gazing into the curiously authoritative Potter stare and met it directly. "I don't know—exactly. I have

137

ideas, some of them fairly detailed, but the picture is very incomplete. I think if you don't mind I won't tell you what my ideas are at this stage. Apart from anything else, I certainly want to see her first. I won't, of course, hold out on you indefinitely. But I think I must for the moment. Will you accept that?"

"Yes, all right. I'm very glad you're here, if that helps."

"I don't know for certain. I have had the impression at times that several people have felt that. And yet my being here is entirely fortuitous, and I doubt, to be honest, whether it has influenced the course of events at all. Except in one direction, anyhow. I don't see myself in the role of the *deus ex machina*."

"No, but it wasn't a *deus* anything we wanted. The situation was too numinous as it was. But mere *homo sapiens* doesn't come amiss. And I'm glad about the one direction, anyway. So long as you're sound."

"I'm sound," said John. "It's only that I don't feel *sapiens*. Far from it. But I must go on as best I can."

"Right. Let me know when there's anything I can do. Shall I tell my mother you're here?"

"Yes, please, if you would. And—get her to see me if you can, will you?"

Derek nodded and went. John waited, looking out through the open door across the wide stretch of green to the belt of trees that bordered the road. He heard footsteps behind him and turned with a question on his lips. It was Richard Garstin, not Derek. The thin, malleable face was colorless and drawn and the eyes blank with inexplicit pressures. The eyes widened at the sight of him, and the lips drew back in what was neither a smile nor a snarl. It was more like the momentary rictus of a man already in pain when the pain jabs him more sharply. John drew back instinctively from the course of the quick, compulsive steps. He started to produce a conventional greeting, but Garstin was already half out of the door. He watched him go, and

138

then turned to find Derek behind him. Derek's eyes, carefully expressionless, held his. "My mother will see you," he said. "In her room."

John nodded and went upstairs. He tapped at the door, heard nothing, waited a moment and then went in. The room was full of the dull daylight. Mrs. Garstin lay flat on her back in the middle of the huge bed with her hands at her sides. She did not move at all. The tawny hair was spread loose on the pillow and from the middle of it she stared up at the ceiling. John, looking down at her, thought she was the most enchanting single thing he had ever seen.

She did not move her eyes to look at him. She said, "Mr. Smith?" as if she was a blind woman who had heard someone come into the room. "Derek said you wanted to speak to me."

He said, "Yes," still standing there and looking down at her.

"What do you want to speak to me about?" Nothing moved but her mouth. He had the feeling that there was a palpable barrier between them, through which they whispered like confessor and penitent.

"About yesterday." He was actually whispering now, kneeling by the side of her bed and whispering at that little sharp-cut profile turned up to the ceiling. She opened her lips as if to speak, but swallowed and said nothing.

"When did the vicar ask you to light the fire?"

She answered quite readily, but speaking so low that he had to bend forward to catch what she said. She said, "Two days ago. Three. Two days before the festival."

"Did you tell anyone you were going to?"

The whole body jerked convulsively, like a patient under shock therapy. "No," she said. "No, no, no. Only Father knew. Everybody thought he was going to." She spoke louder, but still straight at the ceiling. He had never attended a spiritualistic seance, but the feeling that he was questioning a mind en-

139

tranced was very strong. He said, "Why?" He said it sharply, striking down at the lurking, cagey mind, as if to force it to come out of its hiding place and speak for itself.

She said, "Why? Why?" and then suddenly whipped around in the bed. Her bare arms went around his neck, and she flung herself against him, burying her face on his shoulder. He had seen children do the same thing, smothering a question by physical contact, as a boxer gets inside an attack he cannot fight off at arms' length. So much, in a detached, helpless sort of way, his reason apprehended, but reason could not make itself heard in the immediate clamor of the senses. He held her close, feeling down with his lips through the dark mass of her hair, seeking the averted face. She lifted her face suddenly and kissed him. Then the whole face contorted, as if with a spasm of physical pain, and she flung away from him across the bed, and lay with her back to him and her face buried in the pillow. He thought for a moment she was crying, but there was no movement of the shoulders. She lay perfectly still, hidden from him in her own sightlessness, daring him to flush her out of her hiding place and set her running again before his questioning.

He said desperately, "I must know. I must know, don't you see? Someone tried to kill you. You know that, don't you? That is, if they knew it was you who were going to light the fire. Otherwise— But you must tell me."

He broke off, staring at the smoothness of her shoulders, and suddenly she spoke up in a small flat voice without turning to him or moving at all. She said, "No one tried to kill me. The fire exploded, but Father called me back in time, and I wasn't hurt. No one tried to kill me, but Father saved me from being hurt. He had a warning and he called me back." She must have had her mouth clear of the pillow. The words came with perfect distinctness, but indirectly, reflected off the pillow close against her face. If he had been standing up, he could hardly have heard them.

140

He said, "Warning? Who warned him?" She said nothing and he whispered fiercely at the back of the dark, downturned head. "Who warned him?" he said.

She said, "God warned him." She said it in the same small, toneless voice, like a child repeating its catechism, not disbelieving it, but concerned mainly to propitiate authority by getting it right.

John looked at her in silence. He had the absolute conviction that he had only to reach out and take her in his arms and she would come to him, and a great part of him wanted desperately to do just that and let the rest go. As it had once before, something intervened. Pride, obstinacy, a small, irritable masculine conviction that he was being made a fool of—he did not try to identify it. He put his weight on his elbows where they rested on the edge of the bed and got quietly to his feet. The mere increase in the distance between them gave his mind a sharper focus. He stood there, armed suddenly with a new determination to pit his wits against the irrationalities arrayed against him. Let the other side make the next move. He could wait.

He waited, unrelentingly, almost mischievously conscious of the tension slowly accumulating in the great colorless room. An infinitely small, spasmodic twitch of the white shoulders gave him the signal. With deliberate, consciously ridiculous cunning, he walked quietly to the door and stood for a minute with his back to it, still watching the figure on the bed. Then, without turning, he reached a hand behind him, turned the handle, opened the door a little way, held it for a second or two and then, gently but decisively, shut it. For a moment nothing happened. Then Mrs. Garstin turned and sat up. Her hands came up, flinging the hair clear of her face, and froze there. Her mouth opened in a little gasp and her wide-open eyes stared into his. Her arms, white against the dark mass of hair, framed her face like wings, and the upward pull of the muscles drew up the small but beautiful breasts under her high-necked nightdress.

141

She was a figure of enchantment, but he smiled with a sort of schoolboy triumph into her startled eyes.

He walked slowly to her, holding her eyes with his, and sat down at the foot of the bed. "Now tell me," he said.

She said, "I thought you'd gone." He made no comment, but sat there, still looking at her. Even now the proximity was dangerous and he dared not commit himself. She said, "What do you want? Oh, what do you want?" Her voice wobbled despairingly. One thing she knew he wanted, and this he knew she was prepared to give him. The fact that he would not take it, that he wanted something else as well, laid open her defenses almost to breaking point, and he was conscious, even among the welter of his emotions, of a vein of pure compassion for her helplessness.

He said, "Why are you doing this? Why do you want to give Father Freeman all this money? You know you mustn't."

He found, as he had found once before, that he was talking to her as he would talk to a child, and the sheer incongruousness of it startled him. She brought her arms down slowly and then, with a sudden movement, gathered the bedclothes round her to her chin and drew her knees up under them. She sat there, staring at him over the hump of eiderdown, so that the effect of childishness, still palpably unconscious, was almost grotesquely strong.

She said, "I don't—" and then stopped, licking her lips, her eyes wide with fright at what she had been about to say.

"If you don't want to," said John, "you don't have to. Father Freeman has no right to ask for it. There are other people to consider. You know that. It's wrong even to think of it. And I believe it's dangerous. You must tell Father Freeman that you can't and won't, and you must tell everybody else that you have told him. Then perhaps there'll be no more accidents." Her eyes wavered from his, first to one side and then to the other, as if she was looking for a way of escape, but she said

142

nothing. "Look," he said, "shall I speak to him?"

Her hands came out and clutched desperately at the bedding around her knees. "Oh no," she said. "No, no, no, you mustn't. What would I do then? I'd be lost, lost. You don't understand. You're not— You mustn't do that. Promise me you won't do that."

The terror was so manifest that he had no alternative. "All right," he said. "I can't promise I won't talk to Father Freeman, but I promise I won't tell him I've seen you or say anything to him on your behalf. Will that do?"

She gave him suddenly the ghost of a smile. "That's right," she said. "Now go, please. I can't—" She shook her head, looking at him still over the top of her hunched knees.

Now that there was nothing more to play for, the thought of leaving her was almost intolerable to him. He got up slowly from where he sat, meaning to move to the door, and moved instead toward the small figure bundled against the pillows at the top of the bed. She watched him come, with something of her old assurance in her half-smile, but when he stooped over her, she did not move. She said again, "Go, please" almost in a whisper, and he straightened up with a jerk, and turned away from her and walked to the door. He opened it and stood there for a moment looking back at her, but she did not turn her head. She was staring straight ahead of her, and he thought her lips moved as if she was speaking very softly. But not to him. He shut the door behind him and went down the great oak stairs into the empty hall.

There was no sign of Derek. He was glad of that. He did not want to see him now. He went out of the door and down the steps to his car. He was halfway to the lodge gates when he met the small saloon coming up the drive. It slowed and then, as if to make sure of him, pulled out slightly and stopped in front of him. Sheila Drew got out and walked over to him.

She said, "How is Mrs. Garstin? Did you see her?"

The frontal assault, he knew, was Sheila Drew's way. Garstin had told her he was waiting to see his wife, and she had come straight along to find out, if she could, whether he had done so and with what result. Whether this directness masked a greater subtlety he did not know. She seemed a woman impatient of pretenses, but she had the strength and the intelligence to master her impatience if her interests required it. But mainly he felt that she wanted above all to know. He said, "Yes. She seems to be all right."

"Were you up on St. Anne's Hill last night?"

"I was, yes."

"I was in Frantham. What happened? No one seems to say."

"There was an explosion of some sort when Mrs. Garstin lit the fire. She might have been very badly burned, I think. But she slipped on the steps and fell a moment before it happened. She wasn't touched, in fact. But shocked, of course."

The gray eyes were wide open, but the eloquent, mobile mouth was drawn hard. Not for him, today, the brilliant smile. She said, almost under her breath, "A moment before it happened." Her eyes dropped, considering this, and then came up and held his again. "Fell how?" she said. "What made her fall?" It was breathtaking in its undisguised exasperation. It was as if a train had been late, and she had lost a connection. Or even, he thought, as if the grocer had run out of her favorite coffee, and now the shops were shut. He visualized, for the first time with any coherence, what would have happened if Mrs. Garstin had not fallen when she had. He saw the small solitary figure wrapped instantaneously in that searing rush of orange flame and falling then, when it was too late, over and over on the turf, screeching, blackened and abominable. He was surprised to find his voice so even. He said, "I think the vicar called out to her, and she turned and missed her footing on the step."

144

Sheila Drew nodded. "The vicar?" she said. The moment of her naked exasperation was past, but he could not get the horror out of his mind.

She said, "What does Mrs. Garstin say?"

"About what?" Hostility made him abrupt, but she did not notice it, or brushed it aside with a return of her characteristic impatience.

"Well—about the accident. What does she think happened?"

"I don't know. She didn't say much."

"What do you think, then?"

He said again, "About what?" and this time she could not miss the hostility. She smiled at him suddenly. For all his indignation, he felt the charm of it and knew that it was, in its way, a real warmth. "I'm sorry," she said. "You're an admirer of hers, aren't you? It must be upsetting for you. But I mean—what made the fire do that? Had Elias overdone the paraffin?"

"I don't know. Why was it Mrs. Garstin who lit the fire, do you know?"

She took the counter-attack perfectly cheerfully. "I don't know," she said. "I should have thought the vicar would do it himself. It's never been made such a thing of before—so much a ceremony, I mean. I think Elias generally lit his own fire. But once the vicar had taken over, I'd have expected him to do it, wouldn't you?"

"I wouldn't know," said John. "But someone must have known, don't you think?"

She said, "I think she'd have done whatever the vicar asked her. But she doesn't say?"

"I've told you. She doesn't say much at all. But if you're going up to the house, perhaps you can ask her yourself."

"I'm not going up to the house."

"Then perhaps you'll let me get my car out."

She hesitated, even then, about letting him go. She had no tactical pretenses at all, he thought; everything was frighteningly oversimplified. She would not be an easy woman to deal with, not in any capacity.

Finally she said, "Yes, all right." She went back to her car, started it and ran it in to her side of the drive. John started up and drove slowly past her. She was working on something in her own mind and hardly looked at him. Erect at the wheel, her dark, piled-up hair sleek on her confidently tilted head, she waved a white hand as he went by.

146

CHAPTER 16

JOHN PULLED down the steamed-up window and looked out.
There was fog in the air and smoke in the fog. Everything he
saw through it looked damp and almoｳt black. Vast walls of
blackened stone shut in the station beyond the vista of plat-
forms. A sign almost in front of him said BARTONDALE GEAR
STREET. The train showed no sign of going any farther. He had
arrived, and wondered for the twentieth time what had made
him come and what he hoped to get out of it. He had not told
anyone in Coyle where he was going, only that he would be
away a couple of days. George Curtis had been unable to ask
him where he was going, and Charles Hardcastle unwilling. He
had not told anyone else that he was going away at all.

As far as he could tell, he had decided to come to Bartondale
before he left the house at Upsindon. Certainly before he had
met Sheila Drew. He could still hear Mrs. Garstin, sitting
humped in her huge bed with her hands clutching the bedclothes around her knees, say, "What would I do then? I'd be
lost, lost." That had been the moment. There had been something about her just then that had come from a very long way
back, and had affected him like her cry of "It isn't fair" just
after he had first kissed her. The assured, breathtaking lady of
Upsindon was vulnerable, as her son had said; and the vulnera-
bility did not spring from anything at Coyle, even if at least one
person there seemed to be exploiting it. But no one he had

147

talked to at Coyle knew anything about the time before Coyle, about Mary Whatever-she-was who had been chosen by Gerald Potter of Bartondale to share his rich present and expanding future. She had come to Upsindon as Lady Potter, equipped with everything but tradition, and in defiance of tradition had done very well. At least until Sir Gerald died. It was after that, he thought, that things had started to go wrong. She had not found it in her to go on alone, and had made a marriage of convenience that had turned out anything but convenient. She had, perhaps even by the mere marriage, set in train processes that might yet undo her completely. And she had alienated her son, who could by now, from his position of emotional detachment, have supplied the protective intelligence she had lost when his father died. She had weakened her whole position at Coyle, and so made herself vulnerable to some sort of threat that had always been there. That at any rate was what he suspected and had come to Bartondale to confirm if he could. He still did not know how to set about it. For a start he must get out of the train. He pushed the window up and set about ridding himself, as far as possible, of the clinging aftereffects of a night spent in his clothes. He longed desperately for a bath, but did not see where, at this hour, he was going to get one. From what he could see of Bartondale he did not much care for it.

Breakfast improved his outlook and gave him fresh resolution. He left his suitcase in the cloakroom and an illogical amount of his remaining misgivings with it. He was unencumbered and had the day before him. He bought a copy of the *Bartondale Chronicle* from the bookstall and walked out of the station. Bartondale was still dun-colored and damp, but it was wide and airy, and everything moved fast. He wondered what had gone on in Sir Gerald Potter's head when he had exchanged this swift urban desolation for the timeless rural urbanity of Upsindon. A vast step. He wondered, momentarily, whether the shock had killed him, but he did not think so. The Potters were made of sterner stuff. But his young wife—quite young she must have been then—had she been bred in this turmoil, and was there something in it which, even in the remote southwest, she could not escape from?

The policeman looked taller and solider than even London policemen, and had unfamiliar metalwork on his helmet, but he understood John's English and regarded him with a kind of dark tolerance. The *Chronicle* offices were up a narrow clanging side street, all metal-framed windows in black stone walls. Only the newest building here was not of stone, and even the concrete and glass was coming down to the color of the rest. He asked for, and got, the file of early 1960. He spread it on the long table and began to work through it in the filtered gray daylight, while the presses rumbled and clanged in the heart of the building and the traffic growled outside. He saw the news story before the obituary. There was a front-page paragraph under the heading *Death of Sir Gerald Potter*. It said next to nothing, but directed him to an obituary notice on an inside page. He read steadily from the beginning, regardless of the stern national tradition that relegates the wife, or wives, and children to the last sentence. It was an interesting production. The top of the column was the standard thing, kept up to date from the time when Gerald Potter first rated an obituary and ready for use when needed. Then the style changed abruptly, and the rest was warmer stuff, clearly a personal appraisement of the sort *The Times* would publish a couple of days later and print over initials or under the heading *A correspondent writes*— The picture that emerged was much what he had imagined. A formidable man, not unloved, but undisguisably by natural endowment a cut above his background and his fellow industrialists. Only the writer, whoever he was, had known him at close quarters and missed him. Here, at last, it was, abruptly and uninformatively.

149

A passing reference to Sir Gerald's having married a local girl and then the formal tribute. Lady Potter's beauty and charm would long be remembered by all those, and so on. But no name, no "daughter of so-and-so," not even a date. Mary What-ever-she-was was a local girl, but that was all. John turned the file back and asked for the news room.

He fought his way through a series of friendly, not particu-larly interested and extraordinarily busy men until one of them left what he was doing long enough to shout through a half-open glass door, "Jock! Who would have done the obit on Pot-ter in 1960?"

A voice said, "Who in 1960?"

"Potter. Gerald. Sir Gerald Potter of Smith Bannerman's."

"Him? Priddy for certain. He was a friend of his. Why?"

"Somebody wants him." He turned to John. "Chap called Pridham. Not in now. Try the County Arms. Not yet. About eleven. Donald Pridham." He flashed a desperate smile at him and went back to whatever he was doing. John thanked him and found his way out into the street. It was raining and still barely ten. He saw Priddy as a bull-necked man with red eyes and nicotine-stained fingers, re-hydrating himself in a dark corner of the bar after the horrors of the previous night. He had met that sort live as well as in books, and shrank slightly from the en-counter. In particular, he did not want to hear what such a man might have to say about Mary Garstin. A sudden smell of coffee drew him in off the pavement, and he drank it gratefully, full of the mild surprise of the southerner that such details of civiliza-tion should have penetrated the industrial north. When he got to the County Arms it was well after eleven, and he went, un-happily but unhesitatingly, up to a burly man in a belted mack-intosh and said, "Mr. Pridham?" The man looked at him with mild interest and said, "Naw."

The barman said, "Mr. Pridham a'nt in yet. Should be soon."

John apologized and sat watching. He was prepared for anything now, but dismissed at sight the small neat man with a clipped white mustache. "That's Mr. Pridham now," said the barman. Mr. Pridham turned and fixed a pale, rather unwelcoming eye on him, and John, embarrassed and out of touch, went over to his table. He said, "The *Chronicle* office told me I might find you here. Can you spare me a minute or two?"

Mr. Pridham nodded and pointed to the chair facing him. He had no reason to be hostile, but was demonstrably unexpansive. The fact that John much preferred him to the brash creature he had imagined did not make him immediately easier to deal with. John said, "I've just been reading the obituary notice on Sir Gerald Potter, who died in 1960. They said they thought you would have written it, as you were a friend of his. I thought myself that it was a friend's writing."

Mr. Pridham was still giving nothing away. He said, "I wrote it, yes."

"I wondered— I don't know whether you can help me. I've been staying recently at Coyle, near Upsindon. That was where Sir Gerald Potter went from here. I've met Mrs. Garstin. That's Lady Potter that was. Did you know she had married again?"

Mr. Pridham was very watchful now. "No," he said. "No, I hadn't heard. But it doesn't surprise me. She was the loveliest woman I have ever seen."

"She still is. Well—not so much beautiful, I think. But devastating. She's no longer young, of course."

"She wouldn't be. Whom did she marry?"

"Man who was working as their agent. Younger than she is. Not wise, I don't think. That was before I knew them, of course."

"She'd do what she wanted in a thing like that. But it wouldn't necessarily be the wise thing, I grant you."

John made a rather despairing gesture. "I don't know," he

said."I don't really even know what I expect you to do for me. But—I think she's in trouble. And I think—I thought if I knew more about her, her early life especially, I might be able to help. Your notice in the *Chronicle* gave me nothing. Not even her maiden name. It was so uninformative, to tell the truth, I wondered if you hadn't been—I don't know—leaving something deliberately unsaid. So I thought I'd speak to you."

"What sort of trouble?" said Mr. Pridham. He was still completely uncommitted.

"Serious. I think it's possible someone's tried to kill her. But there is an alternative possibility."

Unexpectedly but hearteningly, the pale face opposite him flushed with anger. "Kill her? Nobody would want to kill Mary Potter. I don't know who you are, but you've got it wrong. What do you want me to tell you about her, anyway?" He paused, eyeing John sternly. "Let me tell you this for a start. Gerald Potter and I were friends. I'm not saying we were boys together, but we were friends as young men, here in Bartondale, and went on being friends even after he had made his way. I met Mary once before he married her. She was eighteen then. Well, you can imagine. And Gerald was an impressive chap, too. You never knew him?"

"No. But the son's impressive enough at times. I can imagine."

"Yes. He's here, you know. During term, of course."

"I know, yes. I like Derek very much. But you were talking about the marriage."

"Well—only that it was a classic case of natural selection, or something. I mean—it looked all wrong on paper, but they both knew better, and there it was. It worked."

John said, "So long as it lasted it worked. Why wrong on paper, though?"

"Well—different abilities, different temperament, different

152

education, different class, different background, different everything. And quite a big gap in their ages, by present-day standards."

John waited, and Mr. Pridham watched him waiting but
offered nothing more. Finally John said, "So you avoided putting it on paper. Who was she, then?"

"I'll tell you who she was. That's a matter of history. If you
want to know more, you can find it out for yourself. She was
Mary O'Farrell. Her father was a local postman. He's dead.
There's a brother still alive and in these parts. James. You'll find
him down in Lackington. They're not in touch, of course. Never
since she married Gerald. But it's up to you."

John got up. He said, "I reckon myself a friend of Mary Garstin's too, you know. I admit I haven't any credentials, but—"

Mr. Pridham waved him aside. "All right, all right, I believe
you. Otherwise I shouldn't have talked to you at all. Only—"

"How do I find this James O'Farrell?"

"I told you. Lackington. Where they all live. Anyone will tell
you. Get a number-three bus."

"All right, I will. And thank you." He smiled into the fierce
eyes and found his way out. O'Farrell, he thought, O'Farrell.
Once more he heard Mrs. Garstin say, "What would I do
then?" and one thing at least clicked into place. Irish, of course.
Not the accent at all, or even strictly the form of words, but the
intonation. Always the last thing that goes, if it ever does. The
pitch sequence that is inseparable in the mind from a particular
pattern of thought or emotion, and leaves the Cornish, after
generations, still speaking west-country English with Celtic in-
tonations. Mrs. Garstin had taught herself to speak, in her curious, colorless way, standard English, but her intonation under
stress was Irish. He caught a number three bus and asked to be
put off at Lackington. Where they all lived, Mr. Pridham had
said. Lackington was street after street of little black terraces

153

dropping down the steep hillsides into what had once been the dales. It was nothing like a slum, but it was dispiriting. All he had to do was to ask for James O'Farrell. He never doubted that Mr. Pridham was a man of his word. He opened the nearest gate and as he walked across the few feet of cement slab heard voices inside the door. The door opened before he got a hand to it.

A tall bony woman with red hair was talking to a cassocked priest half her size. The woman's face, which was toward him, was full of abasement and something very like fear. He could not see the priest's face, but his subconscious mind was already whooping for attention. The woman said, "Yes, Father. I will that, Father. And I'll come and tell you, or send one of the children." Nothing short of prostration would get her below the level of the priest's eye, but she seemed to resist prostration only by an effort of will.

"All right, Catherine," the priest said. "But don't forget, mind." He turned with a small waspish smile on his face and surveyed John as he stood outside the door. John for his part stood and stared back, while huge red-haired Catherine looked nervously from one to the other. Underneath the clipped gray hair the features were almost frighteningly alike, but with all the placidity and radiance drained out of them.

"Well," said the priest, "was it me you were wanting or Mrs. Derry?"

John, out of his mental confusion, came out with his preconceived line, knowing it was already out of date. "I'm looking for James O'Farrell," he said.

"Well," said the priest again, "that would be me, I expect. All right, Catherine. I'll expect to hear from you." He turned and went down to the gate, leaving Mrs. Derry peering and muttering in the doorway. John stood aside to let him pass and then followed him out on to the pavement. The fierce little man turned right and walked down the hill, and John fell into step

154

beside him. He had really nothing to say now. He knew it all. He went on more from dislike of the man than from the expectation of doing any good. He said, "You had a sister, Mary?"

Father O'Farrell stopped and turned to him. "Is she dead?" he said. John had an immediate conviction that he saw the possibility of something in it for himself. He shook his head, smiling with pleasure at the other's disappointment. "No," he said. "But it was your sister Mary that married Gerald Potter?"

"Not married. Not to my way of thinking. She went through a form of civil ceremony with a man not of her own faith. I have not seen her since."

"Your father was alive at the time?"

"He was, yes."

"And you had no mercy, either of you?"

"Mercy?" The little priest exploded at his elbow. "I don't know who you are. I suppose you speak in ignorance. It was not for me to show mercy, nor for my father. Mary knows where mercy is to be found. It is for her to seek it before it is too late. Sir Gerald Potter is dead, isn't he? Nothing stands in her way now."

John stopped, and the other, half reluctantly, stopped too and stood facing him. John said, "I think in fact she may be trying to find salvation in her own way."

"I don't know what her own way would be. There is only one way, and she knows it."

John nodded, turned and walked back up the hill. For a moment the priest did not move. Then, whatever he may have had in mind, he put it aside and went on, past the long black line of little houses, to do what, in the exercise of his calling, he had next to do.

155

CHAPTER 17

JOHN DROVE into Coyle in the black darkness, still full of cold anger but tired and uncertain what to do. He ran his car into the Bell yard, took out his suitcase and went straight up to his room, avoiding the bar. He went to the window and looked out. The tower was still there, just visible against the sky and the yellow lights of Galehanger. He cursed it, briefly but from his heart, and flicked the curtains across the window. He went back to switch on the light and heard, as he went, the sound of hurrying feet on the stairs and the landing outside.

The door swung open almost in his face. Cynthia said, "Darling, I thought you weren't coming back. I couldn't bear it. I thought—" Her arms were around his neck and his anger and indecision forgotten. He stopped her mouth with his, and for a little neither of them said anything. Then she took one hand from his neck and, reaching behind her, shut the door. He pushed her gently before him in the darkness until the edge of the bed took her behind the knees and she sat down on it and then, under his insistent pressure, sighed suddenly and lay back flat across it. A moment later, and none too soon, she said, "No, wait— No, look, darling, I must tell you. I came here because—"

John said, "I know why you came here," but she drew up her knees suddenly and rolled sideways away from him. She said, "There's been trouble at Upsindon. You must listen."

"Damn Upsindon," he said, but the spell was broken. He heard her ruffling her feathers in the darkness, and then she slid off the bed, walked across to the door and put the light on. They blinked at each other in the harsh white light, but he saw, although the body was gone from the bed, that she was still his beloved Cynthia. They stared at each other in desperate mutual identification, and she smiled gently and said, "Oh, John," and he said, "You will marry me, won't you?" simultaneously.

She said, "What, do you mean for keeps?"

"I did, yes. But if you think—"

"No, no." She waved aside the suggested modification. "I think I'd like to marry you."

"Not still in love with Dick Garstin?"

She shook her head decisively. "My salad days," she said. "Look, I think you must see Derek if you can. He knows as much as anyone, and he's been a bit desperate to see you."

"What's happened, then?"

"I don't know. Only that the vicar's been out at Upsindon off and on ever since you left, and Mrs. Garstin's been in a bit of a state. And then this evening Dick Garstin pretty well threw him out, and Derek heard Mrs. Garstin raving at him—at Dick, I mean—and it all sounds rather lunatic and alarming."

"It is alarming. Lunatic, too, I suppose. It depends how you look at it. Where is Derek now?"

"Up at Galehanger. But only passing the time, because he didn't want to be at Upsindon. He hasn't said anything to Daddy, I don't think. Can you phone him and get him to come here?"

"All right. Hold on a minute." He went downstairs and was back a minute later. Cynthia was sitting on the bed, but got up warily as he came in. "He's coming down," said John.

"May I stay?"

"Stay all night if you like. I wish you would."

157

She gave him a friendly smile. "Wouldn't it be heaven? Only think of poor Mrs. Curtis's feelings. Let's see what Derek has to say first." She sat down again, watching him placidly as he paced up and down the room.

Derek looked curiously drawn, but his eye had lost none of its fierceness. He said, "Where have you been? We none of us knew." He perched on the bed beside Cynthia and waited for John's explanation.

John said, "Bartondale. I may have been wasting my time. I don't know. Perhaps I could merely have asked you. But I don't think so."

"Asked me what?"

"Well—for a start, do you know what your mother's maiden name was?"

Derek stared at him. "What—? Well, wait a minute. I have heard it, I think, but only very casually. I don't know anything much about her background. Yes, I know. Fairhall."

"Right," said John. "Then I haven't been wasting my time. Your mother's name was O'Farrell. She was—is—Irish. She was bred a Catholic, I should guess in the most abject Irish tradition. She even has a brother who is a priest. She threw all this over and married your father at a registry office. Her father and brother rejected her out of hand. I imagine she has been trying to live it down ever since. Unless I'm much mistaken, she feels she's playing fast and loose with damnation."

Derek spoke very quietly. "I see," he said. "And Old Liberty's taken advantage of this?"

"In some degree, yes. I don't know to what extent. At its best, she's simply vulnerable to priestcraft, and he has undue influence on her because of it. At its slightly worse, he has some inkling of her state of mind and is deliberately working on it. At its worst, he may know the truth, and there may be an element of spiritual blackmail in it. But in any case, there is your hidden spring. I imagine it's only happened since your father died. She isn't really qualified to stand alone. And her marriage with Garstin has made things worse, not better. To put it mildly, he was the wrong man for the job."

"That's true, certainly. Now—what happened the other evening? Something happened then that brought things to some sort of crisis. But I can't discover what."

"I don't think there's much doubt that there was an attempt at murder. Possibly simply a disabling. Possibly only a fright. But I think murder."

Cynthia said, "Someone tried to kill Mrs. Garstin? John, they couldn't."

"I don't know—I don't know, you see, because of one thing. Someone had it in for whoever lit the bonfire. But most people thought it was going to be the vicar. No one admits knowing that it was going to be Mrs. Garstin. She herself says nobody knew. But—"

Derek said, "What did they do?"

"I think they put petrol—quite a lot of it, several gallons, I should think—in the middle of the pile, so that it exploded almost as soon as the fire was lit. They must have gone up and done it the night before. It could be done."

"But how—?"

"I don't know for certain, of course. But my guess is polythene bags. The kind of thing you store blankets in. They'll hold petrol all right. Say a gallon of petrol in the bottom of the bag, and then they folded the top over and over into a bunch and clenched it tight with a hose-clip. Now I come to think of it, they may have put the polythene bags into something a bit stronger but still inflammable—kraft paper, say. Otherwise they might have been holed getting them into the pile. But the effect's the same. The fire blazes up, because Elias has doped it an hour or two before with paraffin. The heat sets off the petrol

159

and up she goes, in a matter of seconds. And of course, nothing's left of the bags or the petrol. Only the hose-clips. And they were collected from the remains of the fire later in the night. All except one, which I found next day. And that was collected from me an hour or two later."

Cynthia said in a small awed voice, "But it failed. Why?"

John stopped his pacing and looked at them both solemnly. "It failed because the vicar called Mrs. Garstin back," he said. "Something warned him, and he called her back. She didn't come, but she turned and slipped. The effect was the same."

"But who—?" said Derek.

"Your mother says God."

Cynthia said without hesitation, "Well, that's right, of course. It would be. God or whatever you call it. Whatever drives him."

Derek said, "There is, of course, another, more prosaic, explanation."

"That the vicar knew the petrol was there? I thought of that, of course. But if so, he was taking a ghastly risk. I mean, what he did didn't work—his calling her back, I mean. The only thing that saved her was her fall. And apart from anything else, we must assume that he didn't want her dead—not then. Presumably he still doesn't. He still hasn't got what he wants. Or so I gather."

"No. That is, he hasn't got her cheque in his pocket. But that mainly because Dick Garstin intervened practically by physical force. I didn't see what happened upstairs. But I found him and the vicar squared up to each other in the hall. Their faces weren't pretty, either of them. I don't want to seem flippant—I don't feel flippant about it in the least—but I can't help thinking that if the vicar had the forces at his disposal you seem to imagine, Dick Garstin would have dropped dead on the spot. It looked pretty human, what I saw."

160

Cynthia said, "But—oh, never mind."

"But the vicar went?" said John.

"He went, yes. But of course that's not the end of it. If my mother's determined to give him what he wants, a mere physical intervention can't stop her. And I may be wrong, but I get the impression she is."

"Did you see her after that?"

"No, I haven't seen her at all. But Dick Garstin went back upstairs to her, and from what I could hear—I couldn't help hearing it, not until I cleared out myself—all hell was let loose."

John stood still, and the three of them stared at each other in grim silence. Finally John said, "There's no chance at all, now that Garstin's come out into the open, that he can persuade her to change her mind?"

"I should say none at all. I imagine it's put paid to the marriage, but that's no great loss. But it can't change anything else. My own bet is that by tomorrow it will be all over."

John said, "There's only one thing left. I must talk to Father Freeman. If he already knows what I now know, I don't imagine I can do any good. If he doesn't—if he doesn't know the sort of forces he's dealing with—then I might manage to persuade him to hold his hand."

"I don't envy you the job."

"I don't mind in the least admitting that I'm scared stiff. The man has never yet failed to frighten me, and I haven't risked a head-on clash. But I don't think he can do me any harm. And I've got to try."

Derek got up from the bed, and Cynthia, white and distraught, got up after him. "All right," said Derek, "you tackle the man of God. What had I better do?"

"Go back to Upsindon," said John. "And I think—I know it's a ghastly position, but the whole thing's nightmare anyway—I think you should try to keep an eye on your step-daddy."

161

"Yes," said Derek. "Yes, I see. All right, I'll do what I can. Come on, Cynthia. I'll see you home and then get along out there."

Cynthia gave John a despairing look. Then she nodded. "All right," she said.

John said, "Cheer up. This isn't really our fight. I'll survive." She nodded again and followed Derek downstairs. John shut the door after them and came back into the bare, ugly bedroom that he had walked into in a near-coma not so many nights since and that had now become the pivot of his existence. A long gust of wind blew suddenly down the dark street outside, shaking the curtains across the half-open window. He thought, I'm hungry. I must have some food. He stood irresolute in the silence, and then a second gust, much stronger than the first, moaned across the front of the house. It's going to blow, he thought. There's going to be a wind. Then he thought, Food first. He went downstairs to find Mrs. Curtis.

It was pitch dark when he went outside and blowing hard. He had never yet been to the vicarage, but he knew where it was. He had food and a double Scotch in his stomach and a torch in his pocket. He set out resolutely through the empty streets of Coyle, and the wind went with him all the way. The vicarage stood off to the right at the end of Church Lane. In its present occupation at least it was by daylight characterless and rather forbidding, but it was the center of recurrent activity. Between the moments of activity Father Freeman lived austerely and alone.

There were no lights showing, but neither were there in half of Coyle, and the people were all somewhere. John walked up the flagged path and pushed the button of the bell. He heard the bell ring back in the depths of the dark house and waited, still resolute to get at his man if he could, but dreading the sounds of movement inside. No sound came. The wind rushed up and down the stone face of the house and rattled a window on the upper floor, but nothing stirred in the house and the door did not open. He rang again, more boldly this time, so that the long vibration of the bell must have been intolerable to a man determined to ignore it. But nothing happened. Father Freeman was not at home.

He turned away from the door and was conscious with a sudden qualm of the huge shape of the church standing almost over him against the dark windy sky. With an appalling reluctance, but without visible hesitation, he walked out into the lane, across to the lych gate and up to the great south door of the church. The door opened silently, and his torch was lost in the huge darkness inside. He shut the door and silence closed in on him. The wind worked on the outside of the building, but from here it could hardly be heard. He tiptoed over to the narrow door in the wall. Somewhere there must be light switches. He had only to find them, and he could flood the polychrome spaces with harsh light. But he was unwilling to proclaim his presence to the outside world. He felt safer as he was within the small circle of his torchlight. He opened the door, stepped up on to the lowest step of the stone stair and shut the door quietly behind him. He hurried now, knowing that what he had to encounter was at the top of the tower or nowhere and anxious to come to grips with it before he had too much time to think. The door of the ringers' chamber was shut. As he went up the next stage the walls that closed him in emerged from the shelter of the main building, and the noise of the wind was much louder. There was melancholy and confusion in the wind, but not the threat of danger. He did not for a moment think that the wind would bring the tower down with him inside it. The fear that grew upon him as he climbed was not a physical fear.

He kept his torch pointed at the slats of the catwalk, but a

163

reflected radiance picked out the dark bulk and gleaming mouths of the bells. Then he shifted his torch to his other hand and began to climb the wooden steps. Either the wind was freshening or he was climbing into it. It was very loud in the louvers now, and he could feel it buffet the corners of the tower, but there was no movement. The key was in the lock of the wooden door and the bolt was not home. There could be some-one out on the roof. He shifted his torch again and then, with no thought for the noise he might make, pushed the door open and stepped out on to the leads. The wind leaped on him at once, far louder and wilder than when he had first come up here, so that for the moment his desperate apprehension was muffled in physical shock. Then he steadied himself and, lean-ing back against the open door, shone his torch slowly around the square space between the battlements. There was no one there. He and the wind had the tower to themselves.

Relief flooded over him. He leaned for a moment longer on the door, getting his breath back while the wind struck chill at the sweat standing on his forehead and neck. Then he ducked back inside and shut the door behind him. All he wanted now was to get to the bottom of the stair without finding that black, grotesque shape coming up to meet him. He went down care-fully but as fast as he could. Bell-chamber, ringers' chamber, the vestry with its neatly painted woodwork, each in its turn let him pass unchallenged. It was only when he had shut the church door behind him and was back in the windy churchyard that he was conscious of a mission unaccomplished. But he could do nothing more. He was tired and had no more resolution in him. The vicarage was still in darkness, and he did not think to ring the bell again.

He would have liked, now, to find George Curtis waiting up with the offer of a cup of tea, but although the door was open for him, there was no one about. He tiptoed up to his room and, without putting on the light, walked across to the window and flung back the curtain. There was nothing outside now but darkness and wind. The wind might blow till daylight, but he did not think it would blow St. Udan's tower down. Tomorrow, Derek had said, it would be all over. A wave of blackness engulfed him, but he was too tired not to sleep.

CHAPTER 18

LONG BEFORE he was fully awake he lay cursing the bell for waking him. It was a single bell beating insistently, and in his dream he knew that he must leave what he was doing and go and do what the bell required of him. But first he had to find something that he could not go without. Memory of college occasions sent him searching frantically for his gown, but even as he searched he knew that this was not a college bell and it was not a gown he needed. He struggled through into a more recent layer of association, placing himself in his pub bedroom, but distraught for something he had left in a drawer in the dressing table and could no longer find.

He was aware of feet running in other parts of the house, and this increased his sense of urgency, but did not help him to what he wanted. He knew what he wanted now. He wanted to wake up. It was the church bell that was ringing, and that meant it was day and he must wake up. It was a bad day. The apprehension he had slept on woke in his mind before his mind itself was awake. It was not a day he wanted to face, but it was a day he could not neglect. He must wake up and deal with it as best he could.

A door banged somewhere. More than half awake now, he knew that this was not as it should be. Early bells from the church he was used to, but generally George Curtis, long inured to them, slept on peacefully upstairs and Mrs. Curtis, if she an-

166

swered the summons, crept downstairs like a dedicated mouse
and hurried off to her devotions without waking her husband or
her guest. If this was morning, it was a very odd one. He remembered, with a twinge of rueful amusement, his suggestion that
Cynthia should stay for the night and her concern for Mrs.
Curtis's feelings. He was not wholly a stranger to early-morning
alarms in unauthorized company. He was glad, at least, that he
had only himself to think about. Nevertheless, he must wake up
and deal with the situation. But it was still dark, damn it. It was
too early even for a freak service of Father Freeman's devising.
Indignation went suddenly and panic engulfed him.

He struggled at last out of his sleep, certain that it could not
yet be morning. The noises in the rest of the house had stopped,
but there were noises outside and the sound of people running
in the street. It was still pitch dark in the room, but there was
light of a sort outside the curtained window. The bell rang on
remorselessly. It was the tenor bell. Not the bell, he thought, to
ring alone, or so hurriedly, even for the earliest of services.

There was a shout somewhere, and the feeling of terror and
urgency flared up in his numbed mind. He sat up, beating the
sleep out of his head, put his feet into his slippers and went to
the window. The light showed red-gold and moving on the curtains before he flung them aside. The whole western end of the
church was on fire.

He looked at his watch and saw it was a little after two. It was
still blowing hard from the west. He ran for his dressing gown,
got his arms into it and then saw that a man in dressing gown
and pajamas was no use at a time like this. He flung them off
and struggled into his clothes, pulling a thick sweater on top of
them. Then he ran downstairs. There were lights on but no one
about. The street was full of people now, all running one way,
and he ran with them. There were a few standing inside the lych
gate, but mostly they stood solid around the low churchyard

167

wall. For the second time in four days, Coyle had a fire to watch.

The base of the tower, where the elaborate woodwork of the vestry was, was burning violently. The glass was gone from the windows and tongues of fiery vapor poured out of them and licked up the outside of the stonework. The western end of the nave roof streamed smoke into the wind, and would catch at any moment. There was shouting around the base of the tower, and a few dark figures ran to and fro. The rest of the village stood silent and agape, and all the time the great bell tolled feverishly from the top of the tower, summoning help which must already be on its way, but which the unseen ringer could not know of. John, halfway up the flagged path to the south door, stopped suddenly as the thing came home to him. Whoever was ringing the bell could not get down. With the vestry burning as it was, the lowest stage of the stone stair would be like the inside of an incinerator. The floor of the ringers' chamber would burn through next, and then the ringer could go only one way. Upward, with the fire climbing after him. Once the first floor went, the tower, sucking in air from the openings at its base, would burn like a chimney. There was no escape except from the top. He measured the distance with his eye, wondering what hope there was that the Frantham fire brigade had ladders that long and could deploy them in time.

The bell ran out in two quick half-notes and fell silent. There was nothing to hear now but the rush of the wind and the steady, savage roar of the fire inside its tube of masonry. Then the village groaned in unison as the lancet windows of the ringers' chamber showed suddenly red. A moment later one of them burst with a spatter of shattered glass, and a long red arm of fire reached out and was sucked back by the savage inrush of air.

A figure came blundering down the path, black against the red of the fire, and John seized it by the arm. "Who is it up there?"

he said. "Do you know?"

It was a man he had not seen before. His face was streaked with sweat and soot, and his eyes stared in the moving red light. He said, "No one's seen him. It was the bell ringing woke us, and he must have been caught before he started ringing. Where's that bloody fire brigade?" He jerked his arm free and ran on down toward the lych gate. John went on up the path, and then turned off left-handed between the graves until he came out on the west side of the tower. People still ran around it shouting, but there was nothing they could do. The door on the west side of the tower had gone, and the pointed arch of stone framed the inferno inside. The hinges of the door, with the woodwork burned off them, hung inward. It looked as if the door had been open when the vestry had caught. With this wind blowing into it, it would have been as good as a forced draught feeding the fire. Even where he stood the heat was already next to intolerable. He looked at the blackened stonework and knew what was going to happen. Nothing could stop it now. Shielding his face from the heat, he moved in and caught hold of one of the men in front of him. "Get your people out," he shouted. The man looked at him dazed and did not answer. He shouted again, pointing. "Get your people out," he said. "Do you hear? Get them out before the tower goes. There's nothing they can do." The man nodded and went off. John ran back toward the lych gate, and as he ran heard the fire engines clanging at the far end of Church Lane.

Someone caught him by the arm, and he found Charles Hardcastle gesticulating at his side. He said, "Who's up there? Someone was ringing the bell."

"No one knows. Have you seen Father Freeman?"

Charles Hardcastle shook his head. "No one has. It looks—"

They were bundled aside by the rush of firemen with hoses, and John pulled Charles Hardcastle toward the wall of the

169

churchyard. He said, "Where's Cynthia?"

"At home. She's all right."

"You haven't seen Garstin?"

"Garstin? No, he'll be out at Upsindon, I imagine."

John said, "I hope so." The hoses had begun to play on the nave roof, raising long plumes of steam among the pouring smoke. "They're trying to save the church," he said. "The tower's a goner anyway."

He saw, faint but unmistakable, the long horizontal lights of Galehanger hanging on the dark hillside beyond the blazing church. He focused his mind on them, as he had once before, as a refuge and reassurance. Something moved across them and stopped, outlined against them. Up there, above the long line of the parapet wall, a small figure stood motionless and looked down at the inferno below. He knew she could not see him, but he raised his arm and waved to her, throwing a lifeline of sanity and sweetness across what lay in between. That was where his future lay. Nothing of this mattered by comparison. A few tons of misconceived masonry, raised in the name of God and playing hell with everybody near it. Tomorrow it would all be over. He almost thought to go up and find her, but he knew he could not go yet.

A woman screamed suddenly, and the whole crowd took it up, yelling and pointing at the top of the tower. There was someone there now. They could see his head quite clearly in a gap in the superfluous battlements. He was quite motionless, standing there and looking down, as if the confusion below was no concern of his. Then, very deliberately, he put two long white hands on to the stonework on each side of the gap and heaved himself up. He stood there, his cassock blowing about him in the destroying wind, balanced and quite unmoved. There was no mistaking him now, and the village cried out its heart to him from the ring of the churchyard wall far below.

170

Someone said, "He's going to jump," and there was confusion and shouting. A man ran into the churchyard with a bundled tarpaulin, and several others joined him in a race to spread it between them at the foot of the tower. Firemen and police stopped them and thrust them back, and there was frenzied argument and gesticulation. An appalling rending sound from the height of the tower overlaid it and a huge echoing clang put them all to silence. From three or four places in the crowd, voices called "The bells," and at John's elbow Charles Hardcastle said, "It's the big bell, my God. They'll all go now." Even as he spoke two of the smaller bells came down, crashing with a terrible discord into the waiting furnace. One by one, crying each on its own note even in its last agony, the bells of St. Udan's spoke for the last time and came plunging down from their high hanging place. The floor of the bell-chamber had gone. There was only the tower roof left now. He saw in his mind's eye the flames licking up the wooden stair to the narrow door at the top. The thing was nearly over.

There was shouting near the lych gate, and he saw firemen trying to get a mobile ladder over the wall. With a curiously dispassionate calculation he measured the superimposed sections of ladder against the height of the tower and wondered whether, even at full stretch, it could do what was required of it. There was less light in the churchyard now. The main fury of the fire had climbed high into the tower, and the nave roof, under the concentration of the white wavering arms of water, still showed no flame. The base of the tower was a black outline, framing in its pointed openings the red glow of the molten debris inside it. The ladder was over the wall and was carried up the path in a rush that met and was checked by a rush of bodies coming down to meet it.

At the top of the tower the tall figure still stood motionless on the battlements. Then, as the confusion deepened on the flagged path below, it raised an arm and kept it raised. Whether it was a gesture of blessing or a warning signal John never knew. A dull red line climbed suddenly up the dark base of the tower, zigzagging and ramifying as it went. It was like a red lightning streak that climbed instead of falling and did not climb fast. The red line jinked round suddenly to meet itself, and a whole section of masonry fell out, leaving a jagged red gap. Now the red lines crawled everywhere, and the base of one of the great corner buttresses crumbled and rolled down among the tombstones. The wave of men on the flagged path broke and ran only one way, down toward the safety of the lych gate. The village groaned with a huge communal voice, and the line of pale upturned faces wavered and broke back from the wall. Quite suddenly, but very slowly, the tower of St. Udan's began to fall.

CHAPTER 19

THE VILLAGE street was deserted, but there were lights on and doors open everywhere. It looked like a village waiting at night for some natural disaster from which its inhabitants had already fled. Only now it was the village that was safe. The disaster, natural or not, was elsewhere, and the inhabitants had gone to see it. John backed his car out of the yard and drove slowly up the long slope to the bridge over the river. He knew quite clearly that he would not drive this way again, and there was nothing to hurry for. Tomorrow, Derek had said, it would be all over. It was the small hours still, and it was all over already. Balked once, the fire had claimed its victim the second time. It was not in his hand to weigh these things. All he knew was that he was thankful the first victim had been spared. The hood was back, and the rush of air caked the sweat on his forehead, so that it stiffened when he frowned. He frowned as he drove, turning over and over in his mind the things he still did not know.

The Upsindon gates were shut and the lodge in darkness. So short a distance away, and no one here knew what had happened. Or no one seemed to know. He opened the gate, left it open and drove on up to the house. There was a dim light burning in the hall, and when he rang the bell, there was movement inside and the door opened almost at once. Derek faced him in the doorway, dressed and sweatered, with the rings of lost sleep under his eyes and a faint haze of fair stubble on his chin.

"You?" he said. "What is it?"

John said, "Where's Garstin?"

"Garstin's gone and taken his hell-cat with him."

"Sheila Drew?"

"Sheila, yes."

"When did he go?"

"I don't know exactly. Some hours ago. Why?"

John told him what had happened. He heard it out in silence. "Better come in," he said. They went into the hall and shut the door. There was a thermos flask and a cup on the table and books everywhere. Derek had worked his vigil out. He said, "Have some coffee. There'll be a cup left." John drank it eagerly, letting its heat go slowly over his parched and aching throat. He said, "Is your mother all right?"

"She will be, yes. She's in her room. No one's been in or out."

John nodded. "It's up to you now," he said. "I'll tell you what I think, but it's up to you. I'd say get her a good priest of her own faith and let him sort the thing out. There must be a Catholic church in Frantham."

"There is, yes. I know the priest. At least, I've met him once. Nice old boy. Father Joseph."

"Good. If I were you, I'd go to him now, as soon as it's light. Tell him the background and bring him here. If he's any good, he'll come like a shot. Then leave it to him. You're going to have things here on your neck for a bit, I'm afraid, but it won't do you any harm. It's time you did, in fact. Give your mother a chance, anyhow. She hasn't had it easy since your father died." He thought for a moment. "Why hell-cat?" he said.

"Sheila? She's that, all right. You didn't know her, did you?"

"No. I've spoken to her twice. The second time, I must say, she shook me a bit. Garstin's no good, is he, really?"

"Not much. He'd have been all right left to himself. But between the two of them he hadn't a hope."

"That's rather what I thought." He walked to the door. "I'll get on back," he said. "I don't know what will come of all this. Someone burnt the church, of course, just as someone mined the bonfire, but I shouldn't think there's the smallest indication who. And I don't think I'm saying much, for one."

"Nor me. All right. I'll do what you say. We'll meet sometime, I hope."

John stopped halfway down the steps and turned. "Come to the wedding," he said. "But not in St. Udan's, I don't think."

"I agree. I will, gladly. I'm really more pleased than I can say."

"Thank you," said John, and went down to his car.

The village looked much as he had left it, but there was a glimmer of gray in the sky. Dawn never came easily to Coyle. It would not be light for some time yet. There was in fact the occasional figure in the street now. Whatever had happened in the churchyard, the village had to leave it some time and get back to bed. He put his car in the yard and went in at the side door. There was no one about. He went up to his room. The curtains were still wide. The sky above the Gale was faintly luminous now, and against their dark background the lights of Galehanger burned in an unbroken line. The dark tower no longer divided them. He flicked the curtains across, blacking out the picture, and went and sat down on the edge of the bed. He put his head on his hands and shut his eyes. If anything, he tried not to think.

Downstairs a door shut quietly, and there were quick light steps on the stairs. They passed the door of his room and went off along the landing. Mrs. Curtis had gone back to bed. The bells would not get her out of it this morning, nor for many mornings to come. The noises in the street were almost continuous now, and getting louder, footsteps, some hurried, some dragging, muttered conversations, the shutting of doors and

175

windows. He got up, went to his window, shut it tight and pulled the curtains back across it. He thought he had better get to bed, but desperately needed a long cold drink first. Derek's coffee had taken some of the ache out of his throat, but done little for his thirst. He went to the door and then, thinking of Mrs. Curtis along the landing, took off his shoes, opened the door quietly and tiptoed downstairs. All the lights were out, though he had not heard George Curtis come upstairs. He wondered whether perhaps the landlord had come home ahead of him and gone upstairs without waiting for his wife. It would not, he thought, be out of character if he had. He crept down the stairs and turned left toward the door of the kitchen.

This too was in darkness. He put out his hand to the light switch and then decided against it. The kitchen window opened on to the back of the house and the curtains were wide. A sudden flood of light in the back yard might worry the Curtises if either of them, as well might be, was still awake. He felt his way cautiously around the table to the sink by the window. He half turned on the cold tap and then, before it had time to run, turned it off again. There was a light in the yard. It was a yellow, secondhand light, reflected from somewhere else, but it did not come from inside the house. He went to the back door and tried it. It was unlocked. George Curtis could not have gone up to bed. Like all publicans these days, he had a very expensive and highly negotiable stock in the house, and his security arrangements were never neglected. John opened the door very quietly and put his head out into the yard. He heard immediately the sound of running water from the gulley on the other side of the yard. Then he saw where the light was coming from. It came from under the door of the wash house. The door was shut, but there was a dim light of some sort inside, and someone was using running water.

The flags of the yard were cold and damp under his stockinged feet, but it never occurred to him to go back for his shoes. An immediate and ineluctable compulsion drove him now. He walked straight across the yard, opened the door of the wash house and went in. Even so, the door opened so quietly that George Curtis, busy with whatever he was doing, heard nothing above the sound of running water. He was stooped with his back to the door, working at a tap over a stone trough. A torch, turned on the wall above him, gave him enough light to work by. A bottle of some sort of liquid detergent stood on a shelf at his elbow. His sleeves were rolled up almost to the shoulder, and he was working away with a long swab, scouring away at the inside of one of the metal drums. There was the faint, sweet smell of the detergent in the air, and underlying it, already very faint but just noticeable, another smell, which John did not at first identify. At almost the same moment George Curtis stood up and saw him and he knew what the second smell was. It was paraffin.

George Curtis straightened his back slowly, looking at John half over his shoulder. The swab was still in his hand. Then he seemed to notice it there and dropped it into the mouth of the drum. He turned off the tap and turned fully around. The silence deepened gradually as the last of the water ran away down the gulley outside, and in the silence the two men looked at each other.

John said, "Second time lucky?"

The little man frowned at him. He was quite calm and genuinely puzzled. "Second time?" he said. Then his head came up with a jerk. "Oh no, Mr. Smith," he said. "No, you've got it all wrong, I'd say." He paused and looked at John's feet. "Where's your shoes?" he said.

"Upstairs. I came downstairs to get a drink and didn't want to wake anybody. I thought you'd gone to bed." It occurred to him that George Curtis had never called him Mr. Smith before. The

177

formality worried him, but it did not seem the proper time to protest.

"Better go and put them on. You'll get cold like that. Then come down to the kitchen. I was going to make some tea."

John nodded. "All right," he said. They had spoken in little more than a whisper. He turned and found his way upstairs, quietly so as not to disturb Mrs. Curtis. When he got back to the kitchen, George Curtis had drawn the curtains and turned the light on. The kettle was on the stove. He put out cups on the table, got out milk and sugar and took the teapot down and put it on the top of the stove near the kettle. He did it all quite quietly and almost by touch. All the time he barely took his eyes off John. He had a small, worried frown on his face, as if he was trying to decide what to say when he was ready to say it. When he had finished, he went and stood with his back to the stove. The kettle was just starting to sing.

He said, "I never did anything to the bonfire."

John was conscious of no hostility on either side. There was a mental clash, disbelief, a determination to know, an equal determination to convince. But they were concerned only with facts, not with the rights and wrongs of it. He said, "Two fire-raisers?"

George Curtis turned to the stove and made the tea. Despite his preoccupation, John still watched in fascinated horror as spoonful after spoonful of the fierce black dust went into the pot. George Curtis put the teapot on the table and drew up the cups for filling. He put the milk in first. He said, "Mr. Garstin's gone. We won't see him again."

"I know. And Miss Drew's gone with him."

This startled the little man. "How do you know?" he said.

"I've been out to Upsindon. Derek Potter told me."

George Curtis shook his head and sighed. John remembered the first time he had heard him sigh like that. That, too, had been over Mr. Garstin, but the case was clearly different now.

178

He said, "You weren't there. You didn't see what happened. It was quite horrible. Or it could have been. It was only a miracle saved Mrs. Garstin." He considered the word he had used and then repeated it. "I think it was a miracle," he said. "Father Freeman's dead now, and I can't honestly say I'm sorry. But he was a miracle worker. Once, at least."

"How could I tell he was up there?" said George Curtis. "After one o'clock, it was. I didn't think. How could I? All I wanted was the tower down."

"Better tell me. You know it won't go any further. But you and I must have it straight, at any rate. What about the bonfire?"

George Curtis shrugged. "They must have done it between them," he said. "Or I suppose he did it, only I reckon she put him up to it. I knew they had, of course. Only from what I heard, but I knew. And I was afraid what he might do next. It was a fool thing to do, anyhow. Even you were on to it."

"Only by chance. But I was worried too. Do you think he knew it was his wife going to light the fire?"

"He knew, all right. He was the only one that did know. She must have told him. They—they were husband and wife, after all." He stood there, with the tea still untouched, wringing the words out of himself, as if he was determined to make an end of the thing once for all. He looked at John almost piteously. "She was the bad one," he said.

"Miss Drew? She was the strong one," said John. "Bad, I grant you. But I haven't much use for him either. He could simply have got out. Better drink your tea. Had you finished out there?"

"Near enough. Those drums have the detergent in them anyway. Not as if they were beer casks. He wasn't burnt, at least."

"No, no. And you know—I don't think he minded coming down with his tower. If you'd had the tower down and left him alive, you might have had more to worry about. I suppose he really couldn't get down? I mean—he didn't simply choose to go down with his ship? They do, you know, that sort. I must say, I wondered."

"It depends when he knew. It went up faster than I ever imagined. Of course, I had the door open and there was that wind blowing. And with him up there on top, you can't say how long it would have been before he noticed anything."

John walked to the window and flicked the curtains back. It was full daylight, gray and colorless, but quite clear. The wind had gone. "It's all over," he said. "It's all over, anyhow. The tower's down. It had to come down, and the man who was holding it up can't hold it up any longer. I've wished it down myself often enough, God knows. And Mrs. Garstin will be all right now, I think. There's nothing else you need worry about." He went to the door and then remembered. "I'll be moving on today," he said.

George Curtis drank a cup of cold tea. He put his cup down and smiled suddenly in the unsparing daylight. "I'm very glad you came," he said.

John, smiling back, said, "So am I." He went upstairs, washed, shaved and dressed himself a second time. Then he went out of the house and back along Church Lane. They had saved the church roof. The remains of the tower ran down in jagged slopes of broken and blackened stone to the drift of ash and rubble that lay across the western end of the churchyard. The smell of dead fire hung in the air, but there was nothing to see. The notice board by the lych gate still appealed for twenty thousand pounds, but it was only the rumor of a war long over. He turned left and went slowly along the flagged path. He wondered whether Galehanger was awake yet and where Cynthia was. She was at the gate, waiting, and came running down the steps to meet him.